Tell-Tales

Tell-Tales

Women sharing stories
for The Christie

Joint Editors

Sally Clegg - Sharon Goddard

The Writers

Sally Clegg - Gail Gardner - Sharon Goddard - Mary Howie

Elsbeth Linnhoff - Ingrid McClelland - Amy Plath - Hannah Sheedy

Design

Christopher Goddard

The Artists

Nuala Horne - Sara Leigh Kerney - Patricia Linnell - Sarah Poynter

Children's Story

Megan Johnson & Lila Perkin

Matador
9 Priory Business Park,
Wistow Road, Kibworth Beauchamp,
Leicestershire. LE8 0RX
Tel: (+44) 116 279 2299
Fax: (+44) 116 279 2277
Email: books@troubador.co.uk
Web: www.troubador.co.uk/matador

ISBN 978 1784623 432

British Library Cataloguing in Publication Data.
A catalogue record for this book is available from the British Library.

Printed and bound in the UK by TJ International, Padstow, Cornwall

Matador is an imprint of Troubador Publishing Ltd

In Memory of

Kathleen Ashworth	Patricia Grall	Sara Leigh Kerney	Chaz Roberts
Julie Kay Botterman	Anne Green	Jack Labrey	Ciel Ruffle-Brandt
John Bradley	Martin Greenhough	John & Joan	Peter Schneeberger
Sheila Bridge	Stan Halliwell	Brenda Mairs	Brian Share
Judy Connolly	Alison Hill	Hugh Martin	Sue Sheard
Jack Curley	Bill Howard	Caroline McAfee	Tony Silver
Kathleen Darwell	Gaynor Howcroft	Meg McGuinn	Jim Smith
Tom Davenport	Josephine Huxtable	Joan Monks	Val Spillett
Val Dey	Chris Jelley	Harry Neal	Rob Tweedie
Susan Dubyl	Mary Jenkinson	Tony Newton	Susan Valerie Unsworth
Dawn	Lyn Jones	Ivy Nixon	Pauline K Ward
Jane Eyre	George Keddy	Dave Olive	Brian Willcock
Susan Fuller	Joan Kelly	Richard Parsons	Terri Wozencroft
Norma Goodwin	George Kemshall	Stephen Rains	

We would like to thank everyone who has so generously donated towards the cost of printing this book in memory of their loved ones, who have been lost to cancer. Without your support this venture would not have been possible.

Index

Introduction

Every person has a tale to tell, a short story in them, a glimpse into someone else's life and the things that have happened to them. Everyone has a voice, but not everyone has the courage to use it, to tell their tales with honesty and conviction.

We found our voices over coffee and treats at Libby's in Marple Bridge one dismal Wednesday morning in January. An idea was formed when a group of like-minded women friends decided to try to write some of these stories down to raise money for The Christie Hospital in Manchester. None of us has made any money from the writing of these stories.

Sounds easy, doesn't it? The first part, perhaps the most difficult part, was finding what to write about, experimenting with rhythm, style, tone and words to express our stories in a way we hoped would be of interest to someone else. But as our confidence increased and we bounced stories and ideas around between each other, writing and rewriting, we discovered that we liked the sound of our own voices!

So, here are our offerings. We hope you will enjoy them, read them and hopefully, return to them occasionally. We hope to entertain you and to make you reflect on your own lives and experiences as you share ours.

Sally Clegg & Sharon Goddard (Joint Editors)

The Tail of the Rat

My Grandmother was huge. Her house was tiny. Two rooms downstairs were divided by the steepest staircase imaginable which ascended heaven-like to two bedrooms of doll's house proportions upstairs. Attached to the back was an even tinier kitchen with standing room for two, three at a push.

There was no bathroom. A tin bath was dragged up once a week ceremoniously from the cellar, where the coal was kept and the spiders hid, to be filled with water from pans boiling on the small electric stove, one of the few concessions to modern living. There was no indoor toilet, just an outside lavatory or the lav as it was affectionately known, outside in the backyard.

At the front of the house three steps led down to the cobbled street below, which ran alongside the busy main road to Stockport where Grandma would frequently stand at her front door, head encased inside either a "muffler" or headscarf, if at home, or a hat if she was about to go out. Her bosom could have fed a battalion of children She would stand square and firm in her no nonsense boy's shoes, flat and tightly laced. No high heels for her, no make up, just plain scrubbed honesty.

Her welcome was as legendary as she was, whether it was to the five year old boy from number 5, who would frequently make her howl with laughter as he proclaimed:

"Mamma Moult, Mamma Moult! Have you got a baby stuffed up your jumper, same as me Mam?"

As she was well into her seventies by this time, this hardly seemed likely, but was the only explanation the little boy could offer for her corpulence. Even the tramps who regularly came to her door on their way to and from Stockport Town, begging cups of tea and a slice of toast, would all leave with a little something, although she would never give them money.

Visiting Grandma and Grandad's was always the highlight of our weekends. Even as a child, I recognised their material poverty, but they were rich in so many other ways. They spoilt me and my sister rotten; there was always a Bunty magazine waiting at the corner shop to collect, always a chocolate bar hidden deep in the recesses of Grandad's jacket, always a pan of homemade soup on the stove or a cake in the tin.

One of my earliest memories of being at my Grandparents' house is of preparing to watch The Grand National on the newly rented black and white television set, which you had to load with shillings in a slot to make it operate. It occupied a whole corner of the backroom and was the envy of the neighbours. We all gathered around in the semi-darkness on that exceptionally warm April Saturday, the curtains having been drawn against the sunlight streaming in through the backyard window to ensure a clearer view of the small screen.

How I loved these visits. That tiny, simple house, the backyard, even the ginnel which carried the rain water away, bounced and echoed against all the brick back walls of the opposite terraces with the sound of my stomping Startrite shoes as I ran to the corner shop to spend my Saturday sixpence. The Bunty and The Beano (another weekly treat from Grandma) would always be sitting on the counter waiting eagerly for my arrival.

"Hello, love, what's it to be today? Some cinder toffee

or a Ruffle Bar?" Mrs Kelly would ask as she handed the treasured comics over the counter.

But on that Saturday, the attraction was inside as we all waited for the National to begin in the backroom. Several neighbours had also squeezed in to behold the miracle of the telly, although only the family was going to watch the actual race. Nobody in those days would have presumed that they could have stayed for the actual event and now, as the time drew closer, only the family was left, me, my sister, Grandma and Grandad, Mum and Dad. As the adults squashed up on the sofa and hard backed chairs borrowed from the front room, Ingrid and I sat cross-legged on the floor, whilst Grandma bustled in and out of the back kitchen with mugs of tea and deep wedges of home made cake.

At some point in the proceedings Grandad had disappeared, much to Grandma's dismay.

"Hurry up, our Lal," she called out to him through the open kitchen door, using his pet name, "or you'll miss't race."

Tall and lean, no one could have contrasted more starkly with his wife if he had tried. With sheets of neatly folded newspaper in hand, he had gone for his visit down the yard, through the sunshine to the lavatory, which was permanently dark because, even in the early 1960's, it had no electricity.

"Lal, hurry up, they're paradin' the horses," Grandma called out again to the small stone outhouse attached to the back wall of the kitchen.

It was just about then that total chaos broke out as Grandad came rushing out of the lavatory, shouting copious words of abuse, with his trousers half wrapped around his ankles, quickly followed by a huge black rat! The poor rat was terrified and scurried up the yard to find refuge in the only other dark place on that unusually sunny spring day: the bin shed which stood at the top of the yard before the gate opened onto the communal ginnel.

3

"Quick, get the shovel, Mary, there's a bloody rat out here," he shouted to Grandma.

With this, she rushed back into the house and down the cellar steps to obtain the aforementioned weapon of choice. She emerged, brandishing the shovel gladiatorially in both hands before her. With an unusual dark edge to her voice, she declared, "We'll have the bugger now!"

So many swear words within the space of a minute in a house where normally not even a cross word, let alone a swear word, was ever heard!

The horse race temporarily forgotten, Grandad came down the yard, taking the spade from Grandma, whilst at the same time attempting to fasten his belt from the rapidly retrieved trousers. Tentatively, he pulled the dustbin aside whilst we all stood at the opposite end of the yard, waiting with bated breath as, thrusting the shovel before him, he edged it towards the back of the bin store.

"Be careful," roared my father, grinning from ear to ear mischievously, "they go for the throat!"

The by now very terrified rat emerged and, with its escape route blocked off by Grandad, flew back down the yard towards us and the safety of the lav once again, accompanied by a cacophony of delighted shrieks and screams from the onlookers as Grandad ran after it with the spade.

"We've got it now! It's cornered!" This man, who was normally so mild mannered and placid, stood squarely before the lav door, panting heavily as if there was at least a rabid dog or a lion captured within.

"We've got it now!" he declared again, as if to reassure himself.

Oh what larks, such wholesome family fun and entertainment. We all squealed and shouted with the fuss of it and by now several heads of the neighbours had appeared over the adjoining yard walls to see what was happening.

"What is it, Mr Moult? What's amiss?" shouted Mrs Crawley, toothlessly from next door. Frantically gumming her mouth open and closed like some strange fish out of water, she stood a picture of Northern caricature, completed by her head encased in curlers and crepe headscarf.

"A rat! That big black one Dick Wells said he's seen next door."

"Eeh, I never...John! John! Come quickly," she called to her own backdoor, "Mr Moult's got that rat cornered."

But what should we all do now? Grandma sidled warily up to Grandad, as if the rat could escape from behind the closed door. Touching his back tentatively but pushing him forward at the same time, she said, "You'll have to kill it now, our Lal."

"All right, all right, I know I will. I'm just thinking on how best to do it. You 'ave a go if you think you can do better."

With this declaration, a rare silence descended as no one else volunteered for the task in hand.

"Open the gate, our Walter," Grandad called out to my father, "best give it an escape route."

"They can go for the throat if they're cornered you know," called Mrs Crawley, unhelpfully, repeating what she had heard from the safety of the adjoining high brick wall.

Dad ran up the yard, clearly enjoying the drama of the occasion and lifted the latch on the gate at the top of the yard, which opened onto the ginnel dividing the terraces.

"Mind it doesn't come round here," called Mrs Crawley, mouth gumming away frantically.

"You mind your nerves now, Mrs Crawley," Grandma called, "we don't want you tekin' a turn. You keep well back."

Grandad now reached forward to the door latch, accompanied by an audible intake of breath from the gathered crowd of onlookers.

Suddenly he stopped, poised with hand on door, "Best get the littleuns indoors, Mary," and so saying, we were shooed inside where we rapidly dragged a chair to the window to continue watching from the safety of the backroom.

"Are we all well back?" called Grandad. "Right. I'm opening the door."

The door was slowly eased open and, after what seemed a lifetime of waiting, a huge anti-climax descended as nothing happened. Nothing emerged, only the dark recesses of the toilet.

"Is it there?" Grandma whispered.

"Can you see it?" called Mrs Crawley softly.

"Be careful, don't take any risks, Lal."

Grandad took a tentative step into the gloom.

"I think it's gone."

"Don't be daft. Gone? Gone where?"

"How the hell do I know but I can't see it."

With some relief, everyone relaxed. My father moved in now.

"It's true, really, nothing's there."

No sooner had he spoken than the rat shot out and it was indeed truly huge! Fat on all the backyard pickings left out for the birds, it paused for a second to take in this human audience and, for a moment, I wondered who was really entertaining whom here.

"Quick!" screamed Mrs Crawley, visibly palpitating now, clutching her handkerchief to her mouth to hide her trembling lips, "Hit it now, Mr Moult...NOW!" she commanded. "Don't let it get away. It might come round here."

Grandad now sprang into action and pandemonium ensued once more, with the crowd cheering from the sidelines, as more and more neighbours gathered to see what all the fuss was about.

But the rat was wise and quicker than Grandad. Sensing its mortality it scurried off, hugging the wall and shot under the gate and, by the time Grandad had opened the gate and rushed out into the alley, the rat was long gone.

We all made our way back to the house, somewhat disappointed, as Grandma suddenly called out, "The race! The race! Quick, we might just catch the ending!"

And with this, we all ran back into the backroom as the horses raced on towards the finish.

"And it's Merriman in the lead at Valentine's," shouted the commentator. "Yes, it's going to be a close finish, but he is beginning to tire with that extra stone on his back."

"That's my horse! That's the one, the grey!" shouted Grandma, pointing at the telly and, as we all jumped up and down, Nicolaus Silver raced forward and took the finish by five lengths.

"I told you I would win, I knew it, I'm always lucky on The National."

And it was true. She never gambled except on that one race, once a year, and she rarely backed a loser.

What a race! What a day!

The tale of the rat would grow to bubonic proportions over the following years. The rat, although truly large, grew first to the size of a large cat, and later reaching the proportions of a large dog! Grandad's bravery was trotted out regularly, as he filled out the part of the tale that only he had truly known.

So quiet and reticent a man normally, he became quite the entertainer when he was called upon to tell his part in the escapade.

"Well, I just went out to the lav., you see and I'd just settled down for a quiet five minutes, when I heard summat move in't corner. Well, I thought it were our Kelly."

Kelly was Mrs Crawley's ginger Manx cat, but it lived more often at Grandma and Grandad's where it knew it was always assured of a warm welcome and fresh food, like everyone else in the neighbourhood.

"So I put me 'and out and gave Kelly a pat on't 'ead, like you do, you know. Well, we were quite 'appy, me and Kelly, me chattin' away to her and stroking her like I do, but suddenly, I had this thought that everything didn't feel quite right 'cos our Kelly doesn't 'ave a tail what with being a Manx and this did! What's more the tail had no fur on it. It were then I thought…eeh by gum…what the 'eck…I pulled the door open a crack and it were then that I realised, as I saw it sat there as bold as anything, that I'd been stroking a bloody rat! I tell you I couldn't get out of that lav quick enough!"

How we all roared with laughter and squirmed with delight at the horror of it and Grandma would punctuate the tale by wiping her eyes on her pinafore and, saying in her broadest Lancashire accent, "Just imagine it and that were when I saw you runnin' up't yard with your pants wrapped round your ankles. It were a wonder you didn't fall flat on yer face!"

From then on, I still loved going to Grandma's but I had a healthy respect for the recesses of the lavatory. The spiders had always bothered me, but now there was something even greater to fear. I would get Grandma to check round the back of the toilet before I would sit down, always leaving the door slightly ajar for a quick exit if needed and I continued to do this for the next ten or so years until, eventually, an electric light was installed, dispelling the gloom and the fear of lurking rats and their long whip like tails forever.

La Douleur Exquise

La douleur exquise; the all-consuming desire for something unattainable; the feeling in the pit of my stomach and the tightness in my throat that I've been suffering from for most of my adult life. Okay, I'll revise that, most of my life in general. As far back as I can remember I have always been the one handing out the hugs in the playground. It didn't really matter who to or for what purpose. I just liked making people feel happy, it made me happy. My earliest memory of a love interest is at the age of seven confessing to the class clown that I thought he was funny and maybe I like, liked him, only to be told that we were probably too young to date. He was surprisingly level headed for a kid. And so the cycle began.

After that followed a string of relationships: some real, most exaggerated, and occasionally, though I struggle to admit this, completely imagined, and every single one of them, assholes, even the imagined ones. But one stands out more than most. From the pile of losers, bullies and frustratingly dull men, one really takes the cake. For the sake of decency (though I have no idea why I should be decent and I have no intention of making it a regular occurrence) let's call him Bob. Now as clichéd as this sounds I knew from the moment I saw Bob, in his slightly too big chef whites, that this guy was something. It started through a window.

Walking past a local pub on a rainy spring day, face down against the drizzle I looked up and saw his face, framed by a slight mist of grubbiness on the glass of the kitchen window. My stomach dropped, my heart beat fast and my hands became damper than usual. Now this always gets me. In any other normal situation these would not be positive signs. Walking down a dark ally and your heart starts racing, you don't start looking around, imagining your new love interest is around the corner. It signals danger, fear; move quickly this is not a good place to be. However, when we're staring into those baby blues and our knees shake we're sure it's a positive. He might be the one. What silly girls we are, or maybe it's just me.

He was cute looking, though not my usual type. I had a tendency, still do, of going after your classic tall, dark and brooding types but his face was light and open, and judging by how little I could see of him he was shorter than I usually like. Not much taller than me. He was laughing, unselfconsciously and I imagined loudly. I think he saw me though I couldn't be sure and I scurried away. Wet hair doesn't really become me.

However this glimpse through the looking glass would have come to nothing had I not met the owner of the very same pub, in that very same week, loudly complaining about his lack of waitresses. There went my heart again. Fate was knocking. How could I resist? I convinced myself that I needed the extra money. Surely to God I wasn't taking on extra hours just to see a boy again? A boy I hadn't said one word to. But I was. Of course I was.

So I started working a couple of nights a week. Long, boring hours in a mediocre pub, with a grumpy boss and unenthusiastic people, but like I had guessed, Bob and I had something. Call it what you will; fireworks, chemistry, it was there. But he had a little something of his own, a girlfriend. You'd think this is where you'd stop. Call the hunt to an end and admit defeat. Quit the bloody job at least. But I was already in too deep, counting down the days until he was single and I was the object of his affection. He did nothing to quell this image of the future. I do have a slight tendency to let my imagination run wild but I like to think that if he had seemed happy, truly happy with her that I would have backed away. I would have… probably, but he was miserable. He said they had nothing in common. He was sure he didn't love her. They didn't even have sex. And so he was so happy to perpetuate an image of a lost, sorry soul, trapped in an unhappy partnership with a mean girl that hardly ever showed affection and I swallowed it gladly, willing to be his shoulder to cry on, shaking my head and rolling my eyes when appropriate, whilst at the same time showing him what a great girlfriend I would be. I spent the hours during and after work making him laugh, getting a beer or two, intently listening to all his stories about his broken family and bruised heart. But nothing really happened until one night after work.

Everyone was heading out after a busy evening shift. Spirits were high even though energy was low and a few sneaky on the job shots had been shared between those of us in the Chefs's good books (he had a secret stash of rum as all good chefs do). We could have wobbled down to the evening's activities, which consisted of band night at the local pub and far too many shots of tequila, but taxis had been booked and Bob, the gentleman that he was, had volunteered to get us one together. We sat close, slightly tipsy and slightly too honest, and I listened as he once again told me the tale of his trapped, lonely life, eyes misting over slightly, though it was dark and that could well have been my imagination.

"We have something, don't we?" he muttered, as he had a habit of doing. He looked at me and my heart skipped. I don't mean in the romantic way, it literally skipped. Had he honestly just said what I'd been thinking for months? Did he use the words that had been spinning around my head? How does one respond to the question you've been praying will be answered? Hopefully with a clever, witty and highly

11

quotable remark and not,

"Yeah, I think so," I stuttered.

Ignoring my lack of charm, he leaned in and I had a few seconds of clarity to weigh up my options. What I should have been thinking about was whether or not this kiss was a good thing. I could already feel myself falling for the guy. A guy I already knew would cheat. That could hurt me. I spent these few seconds, however, staring at his lips and wondering if they were as soft as they looked. Perhaps if I'd thought more about the cons, such as the fact this boy was completely unavailable and had a slightly wandering eye (and hands), I may have saved myself a lot of time. I should have taken a deep breath and told him to stop being silly. But I didn't. I kissed him, and just in case you're wondering, his lips were lovely. Despite everything I still remember that kiss as one of the good ones. After what felt an age of flirting, joking and occasional tea towel spanking that kiss made it all worth it. There was so much promise, a glimpse into what could be, that even though there was so much to say, so many questions, none of that mattered and all those words took a back seat. Who needs words when there are kisses like that to be had?

After that perfect kiss everything else was meant to fall in to place, but instead it started to come crashing down. I should have waited, demanded explanations, waited for the words to form, to erase the girlfriend, put me in the spotlight. But I didn't, and it set a precedent. We'd sit on my living room floor, nursing a bottle of red, and I'd listen as all the wrong words tumbled out of his mouth yet somehow I heard everything I wanted, needed, to hear. I'd make the right faces and sounds to show sympathy when needed. I'd tell him there was something better out there for him. Hinted heavily that that better thing might very well be me, but night after night he'd shake his head sadly, without discussion and distract me with kisses. I'd drop it then, knowing really that nothing would change and I wouldn't get my answer. And I let the cycle continue. I think I was waiting for him to see me

12

as a person, as someone worth his time. I wanted to shake him awake and scream "I'm not your consolation prize." But I didn't scream or shout. I stayed quiet. Worried that if I pushed too much or asked for it all, I'd be left with nothing.

He left his girlfriend a few months after and I still wasn't in line for the role I wanted. I told him he could have time. Be single as much as he wanted as long as he came back to me. I wonder sometimes just how stupid a girl can be.

Reality finally hit the night of my 21st birthday. After a day of bubbles and cocktails, to which Bob was absent despite many an invite, I was left sad, lonely and appallingly drunk, lying in bed, phone in hand, calling the boy that couldn't even show up. To his credit he answered and attempted to calm me down, and in the end my demands were met and he showed.

As his face appeared in the door window, it mirrored the first time I saw him, eyes big and blue, face framed and my heart once again racing. Jumping up to let him in I forgot, as I did often, that he wasn't mine to keep. I held on to him tight, demanding his full attention, as if I foresaw that we were close to the end. My face buried in his chest, the deep throaty laugh from above brought me back to reality, where my head was spinning from breathing him in and probably a little from the alcohol. I was so close to him I could feel his heartbeat. He was warm and for some reason he smelled like home. It was at that moment I came to a conclusion, not clever after a few glasses of wine. I took one more deep breath of him, steadying myself.

"I want you," I whispered, my eyes cast down, my voice dripping with desperation. Those three words held everything for me. See me, want me, need me. I was begging.

He misunderstood, growling and leading me upstairs, kissing my neck and distracting me momentarily but I knew that I had to say the words in my head or I'd burst.

"No," my voice sounding stronger than I felt. "Not like that.

13

You know what I mean. I'm tired of waiting for you. I'm ready. I want you to take me out. I want to be able to tell my family, my friends… I love you."

And then I started to cry. Great heaving sobs that felt like they'd been living inside me for months and they were all clambering to get out at once. I looked up for the first time since he'd arrived and saw what I needed to in his eyes. Nothing. He had said nothing. He didn't feel the same. My heart stopped and skipped that dreaded beat once more. We walked/stumbled up to bed and he fell asleep at the opposite side of the bed. I stayed awake a little longer, still hoping his hand would reach across and brush my back, calling me towards him. But the invitation never came and I had already given too much of myself.

Now I'm guessing many of you have finished reading with a certain disappointment. How could that be the worst man ever? He never beat me. He didn't cheat. We were never even really together. Of course I've had all too physical relationships and I've been cheated on before, but as awful as both of those things are once you tell your friends and you get out of that situation you're left feeling almost invincible. You've defeated something, your own demons, and you're a strong, confident woman. With Bob it was different. I was left feeling pathetic. A dull ache settled in my chest; he just didn't like me. He'd seen the desperation in me and played on it but I'd let him. I'd trailed after him like a love sick puppy and embarrassed myself so completely I couldn't even discuss what had happened with the girls. When asked, "What's happening with that Bob guy?" I simply shrugged and tried not to let the hot, itchy tears roll down my cheeks.

I felt hollow. Someone had seen everything I had to offer and had turned it down. What else had I left to give? I stopped flirting when I went out, which had always been something I had enjoyed. When I walked into a room I kept my eyes down, drawing as little attention to myself as possible. I withdrew from my friends, having once been the loud joker, turning sullen and moody. I didn't feel worthy of people's time.

14

Seeing him a few months later was hard. I heard him before I saw him. His voice had always had a calming effect on me, deep and comforting, now it set my teeth on edge; my skin crawled. Turning round we clocked each other at the same time. He smiled, the bastard. I was furious. I had no idea where this anger was coming from after feeling so empty for so long but there it was, making me shake and clouding my judgement. Almost running, the toilets were a place of solace for a minute or two as I practised deep breathing, feeling like a new age idiot, but counting to 10 all the same.

I started thinking. I was looking good. My hair was pretty shiny. I had a cute dress on. I could win this thing. I stepped out and, as if he'd been waiting, there he was, leaning on the end of the bar closest to the toilets so that to get back to my friends I'd have to squeeze past him. I put on my ice queen face, the one that doesn't get a lot of stage time, and walked with what I thought was confidence, but maybe that was the tequila talking. He grabbed my arm, smiling that bloody big smile as if I was the only person in the world he wanted to see and for a few hours I was back under the spell.

His life was going great and he was happy. He bought me a drink, something he had literally never done before and told his friends to go ahead to the next pub. He was staying for a while. Laughing, we were back to how we used to be, and I leaned in, hoping he wouldn't pull away. He didn't. We kissed and it was just as good as I remembered.

"Come back to mine," he purred in my ear. "Come on, no one can see."

I frowned. Why did it matter if anyone saw?

"You're with someone, aren't you?" He was never a very good liar.

A girlfriend. Again. And there was I in the role of gullible tart. Again. The anger came creeping back and this time there was no counting to 10. I let him have it. I told him how empty he'd made me feel, but how, really, it was him that was empty. He had nothing to give me, nothing I wanted. He was just as pathetic as me and how I wasn't willing to let myself drown any longer. Walking away was difficult. Of course, somewhere in me I still loved him, but finally I felt a little like the old me, that I had conquered something.

I had felt for so long that I had nothing useful to give. I'd lain awake at night wondering what I could have done differently. Maybe if I had been skinnier or funnier or done something differently? Now I knew. It was him, not me, that should have given more and there was no point waiting. He didn't have it to give.

So I have come to the conclusion that, for a while at least, I shall steer clear of boys and work on myself. My heart is locked away in a box filled with bubble wrap whilst it licks its wounds, ready for the day someone is worth my time and will see everything I have to offer, everything I am, grab hold of it and never let it go.

But then again I did see this boy last night. Cute, moody looking… I guess we never learn.

The Woolly Hat Man

Sheila stood patiently in the bus shelter at the corner of her street. It was a pleasant day. She noticed there were bright yellow and purple crocuses nodding their heads, struggling through the rain sodden grass of the verge across the street, tantalising signs that spring was on its way. Today the wind was gentler and although there was plenty of evidence of the recent gales and torrential rain of the past two weeks, at last there was some reprise. Gradually more people gathered in the bus shelter, some faces were familiar to Sheila others complete strangers.

"Well, it's a bit better today," Jenny pushed in next to Sheila, blatantly jumping the queue. She had become Sheila's bus buddy, even though she was much younger.

"Um," Sheila responded, "look at the crocuses, spring's on its way".

"Do you think?" Jenny lit up, risking a last gasp of nicotine before the bus arrived, and she took a long drag on her cigarette.

"Bloody Hell! The bus is on time for once, it's never on time." She dropped the cigarette on the floor and squished it out with her foot.

"Those things will kill you," Sheila said with a shake of her head.

"Yeah, tell me about it."

Jenny and Sheila found a seat and settled down for the journey. Sheila took the window seat as usual; she didn't look forward to this journey which had recently become a regular part of her life. She could think of better ways of spending the best part of an hour, give or take, depending on the traffic. On the plus side it was great for people watching if her bus buddy wasn't with her and if she was and Jenny was on form, it could be quite entertaining.

Out of the corner of her eye she noticed a figure lolloping along the pavement. At first she thought he was running for the bus but he ran on past the bus stop. The bus pulled away and passed the now stationary figure. Sheila glanced back, he looked somehow familiar but in truth it was difficult to see his face. His woolly hat was pulled down close over the top of his ears, his jacket hung off his angular frame and his shoulders were hunched, as if he were cold or maybe he was catching his breath. It was probably the latter.

The journey was slow today. Each stop seemed to involve people with the wrong money needing change, exasperating the driver asking interminable questions about where was the best stop for this and for that. Places that weren't really worth visiting anyway not unless you really had to. Sheila glanced at her watch, they should have been halfway there by now not stuck on Mill Street.

"So, what do you think?" Jenny thrust a leaflet in front of her face.

"What about?" Sheila turned her attention to her bus buddy.

"This," she wafted the scruffy piece of paper under Sheila's nose again.

"You've not been listening to a word, have you?"

"Not really, I've got other things on my mind," she looked at her watch there was still at least 45 minutes to go.

"Sorry, I wasn't thinking," Jenny was quiet for two minutes.

"Well, I think it's a brilliant idea and it would take your mind off things a bit, give you something else to focus on." She let Sheila take the leaflet from her.

"Let's have a look then, I'll just get my glasses," as she ferretted in her handbag for her glasses the bus suddenly lurched to a halt throwing people forward in their seats.

"You daft bastard," shouted the driver. "You'll bloody kill yourself and give me a heart attack in the process."

Sheila's handbag dropped to the floor and people were scrabbling about gathering up their scattered possessions.

"Well that's just great let's add another half an hour on to the journey while we scrape some idiot off the front of the bus!" Sheila rammed her purse, phone and glasses back into her handbag.

"Sheila! You can't say that," Jenny was flushed from recovering her bag from under the seat. "You're not yourself today."

Out of the corner of her eye, Sheila thought she recognised the woolly hat from earlier flash from view across the road.

"Look," she elbowed Jenny sharply and pointed towards the disappearing figure.

"What on earth?" Jenny started out of her seat but the driver had already gathered himself together and the journey continued.

"No bones broken I hope," the driver shouted without taking his eyes from the road, "some people just have a death-wish."

Sheila raised her eyebrows; she had always thought that was an unfortunate turn of phrase, and now even more so.

People settled back into their seats and the rhythm of the journey returned: stop, start, as people reached their destinations or joined the captive passengers still travelling hopefully. Silence was not Jenny's state of choice and before long she returned to the previous line of discussion.

"Well at least look at it, it's nearly my stop, a bit bloody late but I suppose… "

"Better late than never." Sheila finished for her, trying to gee herself up a bit. Platitudes had started to really annoy her.

Sheila read the headline on the flyer.

"Quilting Club! What the hell is quilting club? I've heard it all now!" She didn't know whether to laugh or cry.

"Do you really think I want to sit around sewing bits of scrappy material together like some pioneer woman from the Wild West trying to patch my life back together?"

Jenny hadn't been expecting such a vehement reaction. She had genuinely thought Sheila would have enjoyed quilting. She had joined the club two months ago and found the whole thing very soothing. She enjoyed sorting the scraps and making each piece count in the whole quilt. She also liked the easy conversation and feeling valued and purposeful. Quietly, she folded the tattered advertising flyer and put it back in her pocket. It had definitely seen better days. She was really thrown by Sheila's unexpected reaction.

"There he is again!" Sheila had been gazing out of the window while Jenny re-gathered her thoughts.

"Who?" Jenny leaned across Sheila so she could get a better look out of the window.

"He's the guy who ran in front of the bus earlier, nearly killed himself." Now she could see him more clearly she was certain she had seen him somewhere before but she could not think where.

"What's he doing?" Jenny turned square on to the window.

"Looks like he's up to no good to me." The next stop was hers so she began gathering her stuff together.

"Take this, you may change your mind," she held out the leaflet to Sheila who took it reluctantly and stuffed it in her coat pocket with bad grace.

"Okay, but I won't." She was agitated, overly concerned about the man in the woolly hat.

"Bye then, see you next time," she smiled at Sheila. "Hope it goes okay," she added in a softer voice, so only Sheila could hear.

"Thanks," Sheila too softened and smiled back at Jenny but there was anxiety in her eyes and, as the bus stopped to let Jenny and a few other passengers off, she strained to look over her shoulder at the group gathered around the man she thought she recognised.

The woolly hat man had approached a group of teenage lads hanging about with nothing to do. He looked really shifty, hands in pockets, definitely loitering. The lads appeared to know him; they were talking intently, and then laughing. The woolly hat man reached inside his jacket pocket and handed something over, far too small for anyone to notice unless they were watching as keenly as Sheila.

"I know what you're doing, you tricky bastard," she muttered under her breath. The bus rolled on and she lost sight of the group.

A familiar sight came into view and Sheila stood up. The bus driver looked over his shoulder,

"This one's yours love," he directed at Sheila.

As if I didn't know she thought, but said, "Thank you," in that well brought up manner that would have made her mother proud.

21

She stood for a moment taking in the all too familiar surroundings and with a deep sigh walked towards the building, through the thoughtfully planted gardens that were also daring to show the first colours of spring. She loved snowdrops and as she walked she passed a glorious drift of them, she thought how natural they looked, not, as in truth, that they had been planted with great skill and care. This garden had been designed to create peace and give pleasure, a bit like a quilt, she thought. She had been unkind to Jenny; after all she was only trying to cheer her up.

Lost in her thoughts she had reached the large glass doors which would take her down a long corridor, to sit in a high backed, brown chair attached to a drip which would send liquid chemicals racing round her body to try and make her better. Sadly these chemicals had destroyed her hair and left her with what could only be described as the head of a much loved teddy bear. The nurse had explained that it would probably grow back but not necessarily the same as it had been before the chemotherapy.

She knew the drill but just before she stepped through the door she took a backward glance and there he was again- the woolly hat man, this time talking to a young girl, the same shifty manner, hunched and angular. He put his arm around the girl, she smiled, and there it went, the handing over of a small packet of what? Sheila was convinced now; he was dealing drugs. How could anyone have the brass neck to do that outside a hospital of all places? She was furious. Here she was, about to be flooded with a cocktail of supposedly life- saving drugs, and there he was peddling addiction and death. The strange thing was though she was convinced that she knew him, or maybe it was just the type.

He was walking towards her and suddenly she felt unprepared, she wanted to shout at him and give him a good piece of her mind but he was coming closer and her anger melted into fear. What might he do if she challenged him? If he was cruel enough to sell drugs to people what would he do to an interfering, middle aged woman with a head like a scruffy old teddy bear?

He was standing next to her, opening the door and politely waiting for her to go through before him.

"I thought I'd seen you before but it's strange when you see someone out of context, you know not in their usual place, it takes a while to work out how you know them." He smiled at her and removed the woolly hat to reveal a completely bald head.

"It's my last one today, and then I've got to wait for the results to see if it's worked. That's the killer, don't you think, the waiting."

Then a light went on in Sheila's head.

"Of course, that's where I've seen you before! Here, sitting opposite me in the brown chair! I am a fool." She could feel the blush on her cheeks.

"Yeah, that's me. I decided to walk today. I wanted to catch up with my kid brother to let him know it was my last session and my sister, she's a nurse here. Nearly got myself killed though, that bus driver needed an eye-test. Now that would have been ironic, run over by a bus on your way to your last chemo session."

They had reached the room with the high backed chairs. Sheila glanced at the angular young man, tall, bald and gaunt but with kind blue eyes.

"So you're not a drug dealer then?" she felt such a fool.

"Me, a drug dealer?" He shook his head and with a wry smile sat down in his chair opposite Sheila. The nurse attached the drips and they both sat quietly.

"Trust me; I've had enough of drugs for a lifetime."

"Me too," Sheila closed her eyes waiting for the seeping cold of the drugs to flow through her veins.

"Maybe I will try the quilting club after all," she muttered as she held on to the hope for a future.

Nobody Owns a Cat

Am home

She's still not back.

Getting really worried :(S xx

Calm down will b bck in 10 (: x

Hurry up!!!!! I need you. Sxx

On the way. Love you. B (: xxx

Love you too.

Drive safely, S xxx

Ben's key rattled in the door as Sofie jumped up from the settee. Grabbing the remote, she put the telly on standby as she rushed into the hall.

"Ben, Ben? Is that you? I'm in here."

"Hi Hon, just a sec. I need the loo."

Sofie rushed into the hall and picked up Ben's hoodie off the floor where he had dropped it in his rush to get to the toilet. She hung it on one of the hooks by the door which were already so piled up with coats, scarves, cowls and other cheap Primark paraphernalia that the hooks had long since disappeared under what looked like some obscene growth of modern living or an art installation of dubious quality attached permanently to the hall wall.

Calling up the stairs, she shouted, "I'm really worried now Ben, she's never been away this long before. I told you we should have got her micro-chipped." Flicking her long dark hair over her shoulder, she beavered away nervously at the chipped purple nail varnish on the thumb of her right hand.

Ben appeared at the top of the stairs and pulled off his tee shirt. He held it to his nose and sniffed. "This stinks." Dropping the offensive item into the already overflowing wash basket, he moved into the bedroom at the front of the house calling out, "Did you manage to get the washing power?"

"Washing powder!" she shrieked and just to make sure he had heard her added again, "Washing powder! What the f......" she clenched her top teeth into her bottom lip. "I haven't been able to think about anything except Mrs Tibbs all day and anyway you know I'm clean out of money until the end of the month."

Ben reappeared at the top of the stairs in a clean tee shirt and looked down despairingly, "Hey, hey, what's all this about Soph, come on she's only been missing a day. She'll come back, it's not as if she hasn't done this before."

Thumping down the stairs two at a time, he took her in his arms, enclosing her and rocking her, whilst she melted into him, now sobbing uncontrollably.

"But what are we going to do?"

"We are going to find her, that's what we are going to do. Now, first things first, let me put the kettle on and make you a nice cuppa whilst I do us some cheese on toast and then we are going to sit down and make a plan of action to get our baby back. Okay?"

"Okay," she sniffed, "it'll be okay, tell me it'll be okay, Ben, she'll come back won't she?"

"Course she will, she'll soon be hungry," said Ben filling up the kettle with water and taking command of the situation. "You wait, we'll hear her knocking that door knocker any time now. Wow, I'm really bushed," he says, running his hand through his hair, "I've had a shit day."

Sophie smiled, "She's so clever, people didn't believe me when I told them our cat could really rattle the door knocker until you filmed her that day and we went and put it on You Tube? "

"I know," Ben smiled with the memory of it, "3,OOO hits and rising."

"3,003 now. I've watched it three times since I've been back from work. She's been on my mind all day. I couldn't stop thinking about her and how she might be lying in a gutter somewhere or lost, unable to find her way home. What if she's been hit by a car? What if someone has stolen her? Everyone's been messaging me on Facebook saying that there's someone round here taking cats for meat!"

"Right, that's enough," said Ben firmly. "Look I'm just as worried about this as you are, but we have to get this in proportion, hon. It's no use winding yourself up like this."

As he grated the cheese, he said, "Go and get the laptop, whilst I do this, will you? I've got an idea."

"What do you want the laptop for?"

"To make posters?"

" Posters?"

"Yeah, posters, fliers, you know like those we saw in the park the other week about that dog that went missing. I told you they were proper ass but do you know what? Now, in retrospect, they actually don't seem so stupid anymore. I thought if we made our own poster and put our numbers on and add a description, someone might have seen her and give us a ring. We need to get it out there that our baby's missing."

"Oh wow, that's such a good idea, we could even offer a reward!"

"No, no reward."

"Why?"

"Cos' we'll get every weirdo in the neighbourhood replying, anyway, what the hell are we going to give as a reward? We can't even pay the electric bill this month. I'm gonna have to ask my Dad for a sub again as it is."

"Yeah, you're right, but a poster we can afford, I'll get the laptop."

Together, standing in the kitchen, munching their cheese on toast, they designed a flier to put up around the neighbourhood.

Ben imported the most endearing photograph of Mrs Tibbs that he could find.

"Do you think that's enough?" says Sophie.

"Yeah, it needs to be short so people will read it. Okay you print out some copies and I'll find the sellotape and then we'll go out and put these up and ask anyone who's around if they have seen her, agreed?"

"Agreed."

By 8 o'clock that same evening, Sophie and Ben had searched all the streets and roads in a radius of about half a mile from the small house they had been renting after they had decided to move in together about two years earlier. They had stuck fliers on streetlamp and trees, they had put them up in the local newsagents and the chip shop down the road. Everyone was very sympathetic but nobody had seen Mrs Tibbs.

Deflated and exhausted in equal measure, they returned home

but lay in bed, unable to sleep, listening to the cars rumbling under the window, whilst hoping to hear the elusive rat a tat tat of the knocker attached to the letter box, strategically placed at the bottom of the front door. Mrs Tibbs had initially had a cat flap at the backdoor, but after half the cats in the neighbourhood had decided to join her in the house for a party every afternoon, Ben had had to block it off and it was just after this that she had amazed them both by using her paw to rattle the door knocker, usually just before bedtime. Clearly, she had at first thought this was an undersized cat-flap, but it didn't matter, she had soon learned that when she rattled it someone usually let her in.

The next morning she was still not back, however, and Sophie stood in her dressing gown at the backdoor plaintively calling "Mrs Tibbs… breakfast….Mrs Tibbs," she rattled the box of cat treats over and over repeatedly but, all in vain; Mrs Tibbs did not put in an appearance that morning, that evening, the next week or the week after that and as April became May and May turned into June, the couple began to become increasingly despondent that something terrible had happened to their beloved little grey and white tabby cat.

They would sit in the evenings looking at pictures of her, repeatedly watching her celebrity performance on You Tube and constantly reminiscing about how they had "rescued" her from a very dubious cat breeder in the backstreets of Bolton who advertised on Gum Tree.

It was hard to believe that their precious little kitten had been with them so briefly; it seemed an age ago that they had telephoned the number on the advert one Sunday afternoon when there was nothing better to do than enquire about a kitten.

"Hi, I believe you have a kitten for sale?"

"Yeah that's right," a young girl replied.

"Uh, can I speak to your mum or dad?" asked Ben.

"Nah, you can't, my mum's here but she doesn't speak any English and my dad's not back from work, but it's okay you can talk to me."

"The advert says you want £150 for the kitten, is that right?"

"Yeah, she's really special, really cute."

"But that's a lot of money and we wondered if you would perhaps take a bit less?"

There was a muffled noise as the girl was clearly having a conversation in another language with someone else in the room. " My mum says she'll take £100 for a quick sale."

"Well, okay," said Ben, "can you give me your address so we can come and see her tomorrow?"

And that was how Sophie and Ben ended up going to look at a kitten in a very dubious area of Bolton at 5 o' clock one Monday afternoon almost one year ago.

As they pulled up, they both felt nervous. There were kids hanging around who seemed to be eyeing them up mischievously, like they had entered a no-go area in one of those American B road movies. Rows of modern terraced houses lined the streets in a style reinvented in the 1980's. They knocked on the door with one eye anxiously glancing back at the car to check it wasn't getting vandalised.

The door opened and a small, round woman in a sari beamed at them and beckoned them inside with small welcoming gestures. They entered a very small and cluttered room. As their eyes adjusted to the dim light (the curtains having been drawn against the daylight), they saw a table covered in bright fabrics and a sewing machine. There was bric a brac everywhere, ornaments and pictures of Indian gods, but in pride of place was the most enormous 60 inch state of the art television that Ben had ever seen playing Algeciras television. Sitting in front of the television was an older woman, probably the mother of the woman who had opened

29

the door. It was the woman who had let them in who called back into the house, "Vikram!"

A strong smell of garlic and spices assuaged their nostrils, it seemed to have invaded every inch of the space and got even stronger when a boy of about seven years of age appeared and asked Ben and Sophie to follow him through the kitchen into the yard at the back.

Ben felt ridiculous having to deal with such a young child. Small and dumpy like his mother, he stood very square and said, "You want to see the cat?"

"Yes," said Ben, "er who was the girl I spoke to on the phone?"

"That was my sister but she's not back from school yet."

"Perhaps I should wait to speak to her?"

"Nah, she's probably got detention, but it's okay I know what to do."

The backyard was filled with an enormous shed with numerous cats inside. He opened one of the cages and retrieved a small, soft bundle of stripy grey fluff and put it into Ben's arms.

"She's really special, feel how soft her fur is," and Ben once again felt uncomfortable that such a young boy was acting like an experienced salesman four times his age. Sophie cooed and stroked the tiny purring bundle that mewed and clawed at them, seeking their warmth.

"What's her temperament like?" asked Sophie.

"Er really good," the boy said, "she never hits anyone."

By this point, Sophie and Ben began to get the giggles, feeling the surreal quality that the scene was starting to take. To cover his embarrassment and to try to still Sophie's giggles, Ben asked, "Has she been wormed and treated for fleas?"

The boy looked bemused and replied, "No, there's no worms here."

Ben, after firing off a warning look at Sophie, who was desperately trying to stop herself from laughing out loud, raised the question of the price, "Your sister said 100 quid on the phone but if she's not been treated for worms and fleas, we'll have to pay for that, so d'you think you could ask your mum if she'd take £80."

"No, no worms here, I told you," the boy said, "she's been fed on best milk, real meat, she's ready to go but mum says the price'll have to be £150 but you need to make your mind up 'cos there's someone else comin' in half an hour."

The mother appeared in the doorway and smiling, said, "One hundred fifty, one hundred fifty and you take."

They sat in the car outside the house for a full two minutes before they both capitulated. Sophie pleaded, "She's so cute, Ben, we can't leave her here…please…please… pretty please," she implored, using the most appealing, childlike tone she could muster, pressing herself into his arms with suggestions of affection to come later on that evening. They both knew deep down that it was a stupid decision just as they knew they were being ripped off. Ben decided to make one last attempt at barter.

He knocked on the door only once before the woman appeared again with an even bigger smile on her face; it was quite clear to everyone who was winning this battle at bartering. Ben knew he was hopelessly out of his depth, but he made one last attempt to redeem some remnant of pride in the negotiations.

"One hundred fifty," she stated firmly before he could speak.

Ben held out five twenty pound notes in the shape of a fan and said very slowly and loudly, as though he was speaking to someone of questionable mental ability, "£100, that's it, that's everything I've got."

The woman folded her arms severely across the front of her sari and pursed her lips defiantly, her ability to understand English clearly not in question when it came to the art of negotiation.

"Vikram," she yelled again and, as Vikram appeared, complete with the kitten in his arms, she rattled off to him a series of instructions in a language that Ben had never heard before. Vikram then interpreted her words to Ben.

"She says that's not enough for such a special cat what's been fed on milk and meat."

A sharp series of exchanges took place between son and mother and it became obvious to Ben that Vikram had switched sides somewhere along the way. He clearly realised, despite his age, that though obviously naïve, the couple just might get pushed too far and the sale was in danger.

"Okay this is her final offer: £120 and you can take the cat now."

Ben went back out to the car and, popping his head through the open window, said to Sophie, "Give me that £20 in your bag and we can take her."

The £120 was handed to the mother who beamed and, holding her hands together, as if in prayer, said something to Ben. He turned to Vikram who said as he handed the kitten over to him, " She says this is a very lucky cat who will always bring you good fortune."

Returning home with their little bundle of fluff, they both felt a strange mixture of emotions, knowing that, although they had paid a ridiculous sum of money for a very ordinary kitten that hadn't been wormed or deflead, she was theirs and they were both quite unreasonably and ecstatically happy and proud.

However, after two months of wandering the neighbourhood every evening and putting up new posters as the old ones got frayed and damaged, they were beginning to feel that their luck had run out. It seemed likely that Mrs Tibbs had disappeared for good.

Even Mrs Salt, their elderly neighbour, would stand at her front door almost every afternoon as Sophie came home from work and ask, "Still no sign of her, love?" and as Sophie shook her head sadly, she would say, "Oh dear, well still, no news is good news, isn't it love? She might just turn up yet. You know what they say, nobody owns a cat."

The simple truth was that Mrs Tibbs wasn't just a cat to Sophie and Ben, she was a part of their family and until children would come along some years later, a substitute baby.

By July they had almost given up hope until one evening, driving home after a shopping trip to the local Co Op, they took a short cut up a side street when Sophie screamed out loudly, "Stop the car, Ben! Stop the car!"

He screeched to a halt. "What the….. Soph, Jesus, I nearly crashed the car, what the hell's wrong with you?"

"Mrs Tibbs, I've just seen Tibby," and she jumped from the car and, racing round a slight curve in the road, just saw the back end of a stripy cat that she thought she recognised only too well. It couldn't be! It had to be!

Ben parked the car and ran over to join Sophie who was peering over the low front wall of a semi-detached house into someone's garden.

"Look, Ben," she called. "There, I swear it's her! Mrs Tibbs," she called softly, terrified that the cat would run away again, extending out her hand. "Come here, Tibby, come here."

Ben, feeling like a criminal, ducking low under the window, in case anyone saw him from inside the house, ran into the garden and retrieved the cat, which made no effort to get away from him. He ran back onto the road, still crouching.

"Oh my God, it's her! It's her, Ben, but look she's so thin and her coat looks awful." Sophie scooped the cat into her arms and said, "Thank God we've found you, Tibby. I knew she wasn't dead, Ben, I just knew it! Come on, let's get her home."

In the car, Ben drove with one hand on the wheel and one hand on the cat as they both tried to soothe her, for Mrs Tibbs had never liked car journeys. However, it soon became apparent to Sophie that she really was severely emaciated and half way back she said, "Ben, we need to take her to a vet's, there's that new one that opened a couple of weeks ago up the road. Let's go there now. We need to get her checked out, she looks really ill."

"Oh, Soph. that's going to put us under real stress. How much will that cost?"

"Come on, Ben, this is Mrs Tibbs we're talking about. It won't be much, let's just get her checked out."

So off they went to the vets, where they emerged almost forty minutes later and £65 lighter after the vet had administered an injection and a course of antibiotics. They were to feed her only fresh chicken or fish in several small meals throughout the day until Mrs Tibbs had gained some weight and, he was most emphatic about this, she must not be allowed outside under any circumstances, but be placed in a quiet room on her own in her bed with a litter tray for a day or two or until she recovered her strength. He had also advised that they got the cat microchipped as soon as they could afford it.

After yet another trip to the supermarket to buy fresh chicken, a litter tray and cat litter, they returned home, tired and emotionally exhausted but the happiest they had been in months. Mrs Tibbs wolfed down the fresh chicken and they eventually placed her in the small back bedroom for the night, complete with the newly purchased litter tray.

"Oh Ben, I'm so happy, but I do hope she'll be all right, she just doesn't seem the same, like something terrible's happened to her," she said as she snuggled up to him under the covers later that night.

"She'll be fine, we've got her back and that's all that matters," said Ben, "although I have to say I thought the vet's fees were a bit steep. Crikey, Soph, we're going to have to go easy on money and he wants to see her again next week! I hope he doesn't want another 65 quid. Anyway, let's get some kip, I'm absolutely shattered."

It was just at that point, just as they were drifting off into a well earned sleep, that they both heard the very distinct sound of the rat a tat tat of the letter box downstairs. Ben sat upright in bed. Who the hell could be calling at this time of night? Sophie snapped on the light and stared at Ben aghast. With absolute horror and a dawning of realisation that passed telepathically between the two of them, she ran down the stairs and, opening the front door, stood back as a distinctly grey, small tabby cat flashed past her and ran into the living room.

She turned to look at Ben who was standing with his mouth wide open at the top of the stairs, "That was Mrs Tibbs, Ben, so *what* is *that* in the back bedroom?"

At 8 o'clock the next morning, Ben drove to the house from where they had taken the cat. Sophie knocked on the door, holding the imposter firmly in her arms whilst Ben stayed in the car, looking shame-faced and guilty.

The door opened and a middle-aged lady came out in her dressing gown, looking tired and dishevelled.

"I'm really sorry to disturb you," said Sophie, "but is this your cat?"

"Yes," said the woman, "We were wondering where she'd gone."

She took the cat from Sophie and it jumped from her arms and ran back into the house.

"I feel really bad about this," said Sophie, "but we took her home with us, I thought she was our cat that went missing some months ago. But last night our cat came back and then we realised that we'd taken yours by mistake."

"Oh, right," said the woman, "well, don't worry about it, thanks for bringing her back."

"The thing is," said Sophie, slowly, "we took her to the vets because she was so thin and they said she needed an injection and antibiotics. It cost us £65 and we're really short of money," and she held out the bottle of tablets.

The woman roared with laughter, taking the tablets from the proffered hand, "Well they saw you coming didn't they? That cat's at least 22 years old; I'm amazed it's lasted this long. Anyway, I have to get on, love, or I'll be late for work." So saying, she slammed the door firmly shut.

Sophie returned to the car feeling really stupid and despondent and just to cap it all off, when they returned home, the real Mrs Tibbs had aborted a litter of kittens all over the sofa, entailing yet another visit to the vet's and some seriously unpleasant cleaning up!

Wheel It Like Beckham

Fog and drizzle, a miserable day but ideal for accompanying his wife on a shopping trip. His preferred pastimes of walking, bike riding and golf would not have been a pleasant experience even for a macho athletic type like himself. He was sure his wife would be grateful that he had condescended to accompany her to a supermarket, normally alien territory for an old fashioned chauvinist who bravely kept the flag flying for beer swilling and male bonding in real ale pubs. Not for him the metro sexual attitudes of the younger generation; he shuddered at the thought that if he had been born two decades later he would have been expected to have attended pre-natal classes, be present at the birth of off spring, take paternity leave (perish the thought) and generally be expected to make himself useful around the house.

At the birth of his daughter, he had fond memories of being summarily dismissed from the delivery room as being of no use whatsoever; he was in fact a positive hindrance. He was only allowed to see them again, once he had been fortified by a fish and chip supper washed down by a couple of pints, after which both wife and baby were tidied up in bed and cot. He still found it difficult to comprehend why insisting that his wife assist him with the Telegraph crossword was unreasonable. Fortunately, the hospital staff had other ideas when they were attaching various drips and her arm was beginning to look like a heinous crime scene.

He really would have preferred to have been born a few centuries earlier, been a country squire with a modest manorial estate, wandering around the grounds roggering the milkmaids, shooting rabbits, with a case of vintage port tucked away in the cellar…perfect!

These days he lamented that it was impossible to show appreciation of the opposite sex. What was the world coming to when a man was chastised for slapping a few bottoms and fondling breasts when it took his fancy? His wife, having indulged his behaviour for some years, was conscious of recent social trends and told him in no uncertain terms, that if he did not put a stop to it he would be arrested and, fortunately for her, her lurid description of prison life, was not to his liking.

She had a sadistic method of frightening him into good behaviour, like showing him graphic depictions of syphilitic sores, gangrenous penises and suchlike. She usually provided the pictures just before imminent departures on business trips to Paris or Frankfurt. His enthusiasm for carnal dalliance had already been tempered a while ago, however, after an encounter with a transvestite in the Bois de Boulogne when he discovered "she" had more appendages than he felt comfortable with and, anyway, facial stubble was a real turn off.

He entered the bright lights of the cavernous store and was overwhelmed by the vulgar display of unimaginable choice, the cacophony of ubiquitous "musac". Fortunately, they had only one item to purchase: a television for their now grown-up daughter's birthday. If he could just turn off; contemplate his faulty golf swing, plan a walk, snooze on his feet; it would be over, and they would be home in no time.

His wife, meanwhile, also hoped this expedition would be over quickly as she equally hated shopping with her husband.

It was the way he deliberately disengaged at the store entrance, dispatching his brain cells into his subconscious. It was the open defiance that irritated her.

The television was chosen with little argument; husband momentarily re-engaging with the present and making sensible suggestions before retreating into zombie-mode, as they made their way to the check out.

It was just as they joined a long queue, that she remembered they needed some milk. She asked her husband to go and get the said item whilst she kept her place at the check out. He looked vaguely affronted at being asked to actually do something independently, but ambled off in his semi comotosed state down the aisles looking for dairy produce.

Suddenly, her attention was drawn to the muted but excited exclamations of other shoppers.

Then she saw him. Slim, perfectly proportioned, slightly tanned. He was perusing the C.D. collection whilst a well-manicured hand ran through his shining, blonde hair. A shiver of exhilaration and longing ran through her body. He was beautifully attired, understated and chic. Next to him was a fully laden shopping trolley with items neatly placed in order, toiletries and detergents on one side, food on the other. He had a note pad and had been picking off the items he had purchased. He selected a magazine and exchanged pleasantries with a fellow shopper who had overcome shyness to speak to the legendary football star.

He looked cool and distant, but also had the effortless ability of a man confident in his skin. So at ease in his maleness, that pushing a shopping trolley could not possibly dent *his* masculinity and authority. He seemed at ease with domesticity.

She reluctantly turned from this delicious apparition to look for the hapless shopper. She saw him about thirty yards away, still studying the dairy items of the tinned and dried variety. He looked very puzzled and was unable to understand (being a supermarket virgin) why the fresh milk was not with the other, similar goods.

A small, wiry, grey haired lady of advanced years approached him gently. She obviously thought he was a recipient of care in the community. She surreptitiously looked round for his carer and seeing none, led him by the hand to the refrigerated section. His wife, observing this, felt anger and shame in equal measure at her failure to train him to be a useful member of society.

Her attention was again drawn to the Manchester United hero. She could see him now in profile. In her mind's eye she slowly undid his shirt buttons, slackened the belt of his trousers to reveal the well-muscled torso within. She was just looking forward to experiencing this when her reverie was interrupted by the familiar dulcet tones of her loved one.

"I've got it!" he yelled with forced jollity. She saw him striding towards her, red faced, grinning maniacally with the milk held aloft. It was the look of triumphant achievement that pushed her over the top. He looked like a warrior in a nature programme who had speared a bison on the great planes and was conveying it home for the communal feast. All he had actually done was pick up a bottle of milk and it had taken about ten minutes to achieve that task.

She boomed in a voice Lady Bracknell would have admired, "David Beckham would not take that long to find the milk; in fact David Beckham knows where everything is in the store. David Beckham can do a complete family shop in twenty minutes and still look at the magazines."

The man looked surprised and nonplussed, convinced his wife had lost her reason.

"What's David Beckham got to do with anything?"

She was now in full flow, attracting attention from other curious shoppers, "He's got everything to do with it. He's got all those career responsibilities and still manages to put his family first!"

Thinking she was joking, he warmed to his subject, " Don't be ridiculous, woman, you wouldn't catch David Beckham in Tesco on a Sunday afternoon wheeling a trolley full of nappies and washing powder." He laughed, "Do you really believe that our foremost, international football star is going to walk past us with a trolley full of goods? Don't be daft."

"Well, as a matter of fact, I am."

At that precise moment, David Beckham with lightning speed, guided the trolley through the admiring crowd. He weaved and dribbled his way with expert timing and alacrity until he reached the goal of the exit. He was gone in an instant like a god on a winged chariot.

The husband was in a state of shock, "That ….that was David Beckham," he said incredulously. His wife said nothing, just stared at him and grinned victoriously in that challenging way that was guaranteed to provoke a violent verbal response and it came with explosive force.

"It's preposterous, a man of his standing wasting his time and talent on shopping expeditions. It's no wonder England can't win the World Cup if its best players are lumbered with domestic detritus all day. He'll put his back out bending over those trolleys. He should be where he belongs – on the training ground!"

There was a sharp intake of breath from fellow shoppers as she retorted with venom, "Nonsense. I admire him- a modern man who is able to multi task and is in touch with his feminine side. It's a wonder men like you haven't been put out of their misery, stuffed and put in a glass cabinet in the museum with the Dodos."

"Well, that's rather harsh. I….."

"Stop! That's enough!" The whistle was blown and a red card was presented by the check out assistant, who had decided to referee this and put a stop to the warring pair. Putting all the customer care and training she had received aside, she fumed, "Do you want this bloody television or shall I ask the staff to return it to the shelf. And if you two carry on rowing I will have to call security and have you removed from the premises."

The couple were temporarily chastened and the woman mumbled an apology through gritted teeth. They paid for their purchases and, even as they were sent off and wheeled their trolley to the door, it was obvious from their demeanour that this heated discussion had a long way to go.

They would continue the second half on the way home and beyond.

Sisterhood

After retiring, Lucy told her friends that she and Sam were off to spend three months in Spain. Many eyebrows were raised in disbelief. Some shook their heads and others guffawed. The general consensus of opinion was that she would last perhaps a few weeks before returning home! What would she do? Surely she would have to return home in between? Packing very little luggage, she looked at the small black photo album which she had bought on a whim in the sales earlier in the week. Little did she know that each of those fifteen blank, black card pages would be a portal of inspiration, resulting in a fervent outpouring of artistic expression and a meeting of friends whose portraits would be forever etched in her mind.

Arriving in Spain, the first month had been planned. They would spend time with their friends in Nerja, returning with them the second week to their apartment on the Costa del Sol. All changed as Sam's friend's mother was given three months to live. Sam and Lucy were destined to spend their first month together. Sam was content, but Lucy's restlessness started to uncoil. Recognising this and her own propensity to become bored, she was determined to keep busy!

The beginning of her three month adventure began with her friend Gerri, who lived in the next block of apartments.

Offering to take her to an art group on Monday morning, Lucy readily accepted. Feeling nervous but excited, she walked along the back path, unlocked the gate and waited for her friend to pick her up. Climbing into the car she heartily hailed a good morning to all.

"Glad you could make it. Oh you've brought something with you. Good for you. What is it?" Gerri asked.

"Oh, just a few bits and pieces to help inspire me," replied Lucy.

Driving off, Lucy fleetingly caught Gerri's glance through the car mirror. It was as though she could sense Lucy's excitement and was anticipating the contents of the box. Because Lucy liked to be prepared, and also to surprise, she had thrown a small picture of threads and materials together the night before, entitling it: Spanish Sunset. Thinking about her first piece nestled amongst the fabrics in the bottom of the box, Lucy was pleased, remembering how the tiny snipped bits of golden material glistened against the black background, standing proud of the red, blue, purple and pink threads depicting a Spanish sky.

It was whilst visiting the community office, where Maria worked that Lucy had spotted the gold curtains which, having only slightly faded, had been donated to the church bazaar.

"Good morning, Senora. How are you? Beautiful day isn't it? Anything I can do for you? Is everything ok?"

Maria's dark Spanish eyes shone with a genuine warm welcome. After explaining her artistic plans, Maria readily handed over the bags of material. Lucy washed and cut each curtain into strips, fraying some and making yarn balls with the rest. Whilst handling the delicate strands of golden thread, which slipped smoothly through her fingers and spilled into pools on the marble floor, colourful images burst in Lucy's mind.

Picking up Elaine on their way, they journeyed to the artist's house, which nestled within the hills outside Estepona. Although cold, it was a welcoming house, full of traditional Spanish character. Lucy was greeted with the customary peck of a kiss on each cheek and shown where she could work on the large dining-room table littered with artist's paints, jam jars, newspapers and kitchen roll. She was introduced to Rhianna who made cards and eighty four year old Liz who was a dab hand in acrylics. She said hello to two other girls who being new to the group, like Lucy, had no idea what to expect. Val proudly showed Lucy all her beautiful water-colour paintings of flowers, flamenco dancers, animals and local scenes which were displayed around a heavy Spanish dresser. She particularly admired the small painting of three pears leaning against a small shelf. Little did she realize then that the three pears would be the start of her fruit collection, which would culminate in a variety of mouth watering and delicious citrus dishes. Lucy warmed to Val as she invited her to look through the books. "If you see anything you'd like to have a go at, just tell me."

Lucy introduced herself to Ruth, who came from Gorton and, as a youngster, had played with John Thaw in the backstreets of Manchester. Although in her seventies and a widow, she had become stalwart in her determination to live an independent life in Spain. Whilst sketching away, Ruth reminisced on how she had taken up driving again and regaled her with travel stories about the Caribbean. Buying cheap scarves and small bits of jewellery, she sent them back to her daughter in the UK who sold them at double the price! Noticing that she seemed in a little discomfort Lucy asked if she was ok.

"Silly fool, I am doing the splits getting out of the bath last night. Don't tell anyone though. Don't want my daughters finding out or they'll want me home!"

Later that evening and with great enthusiasm, Lucy told Sam all about the art group. After listening, Sam felt inspired to replicate in acrylics, Picasso's Buste De Femme Au Chapeau, also known as Bust De Dona Amb Barret painted in 1962.

In her mind's eye Lucy envisaged how Picasso would have painted the portraits of the different ladies she had met so far. Susan was in her late fifties and she had met her at a floral demonstration. Being small and rotund and in her late fifties, she reminded Lucy of a busy, bumble bee sporting a Dusty Springfield make over. But she also noticed that Susan was good company and a support to Carol, who obviously was struggling with Parkinson's.

"There's been a huge improvement since she's been taking the new medication, especially driving. You can't imagine what a roller coaster of a ride being a passenger was before!" One could definitely understand Susan's relief after watching Carol attempt to start walking, reminding Lucy of a bull preparing to charge! She pawed the dirt underneath her feet, threw the dust behind her and, with head down, she would determinedly set off, pulling herself upright on reaching her destination and pinning herself to the ground with her wooden, silver tipped cane. One could envisage the bellows of steam emanating from Carol's nostrils at the exertion of such effort and determination. Picasso would have had a field day!

On her second visit to the art group she met Annie. She liked Annie; they latched onto each other. Using an easel, Annie would attack the canvas with large, bold, deliberate, sweeping   brushstrokes and with a creative enthusiasm which belied her age. Annie's perceptive eyes gleamed with a dancing liveliness and an impish sense of humour. She admired Lucy's textile work and, looking through the black album which now contained four pictures entitled: Spanish Heat, Peeping through the Hedge, Mackerel Sky, Red Space Invaders/Hoppers and Frosty night, she declared, "Well, girl, they are good!"

It was the custom after coffee and cake that the art group would look at each other's work. The wonderful thing about this was the genuine and sincere way that everybody commented positively on everybody else's work. The various ladies studied Lucy's work and asked how she arrived at her different ideas. Thinking about her response, Lucy replied that it was when the threads and colours were being unravelled, twisted, pulled and cajoled that the picture's image would make itself known to her. The following week, Lucy felt flattered when Val produced a box similar to her own, brimming with ribbons, threads and wools for everyone to use. She had been further surprised when Val had asked her advice on the material she should use to decorate a cockerel's tail. It was towards the end of a bitterly cold morning and the artists had formed a huddle in front of the kitchen open log fire, reminding Lucy of a winter scene painted by Bruegal, that Val produced from the bottom of her newly acquired box a pair of huge knitting needles. Insisting that Lucy take them home and have a play, she transferred them to what she impishly termed as Lucy's Pandora's Box.

Sitting on the settee she started knitting. On arriving home, Sam had asked her if she was knitting a fishing net and even David, the next door neighbour, had asked her if she was making preparations to catch her own supper. Regardless of the comments and casting off, Lucy attached and hung the net from a garden cane. The two materials which she had chosen to knit with fell away from each, the bottom material being weightier than the top. This instantly gave the impression of a waisted dress. Attaching a cane to the bottom of the net, an idea sprung to Lucy's mind and the piece became known as the 'Sea Fairy's dress'. The dress was adorned with silver and gold threads, antique Spanish lace, burnished gold braids, vibrant colours of teased wispy wools and cottons and intricately patterned shells were carefully placed and suspended within the fairy's French knotted necklace, hem and waisted medieval styled belt. To Lucy's delight, Sam instantly admired the dress and attached it to the bedroom wall. The piece was ethereal; it was magical and awaited the wearer who Lucy imagined stealthily sneaking in one night to take ownership. Imagine her surprise when, walking along the harbour shops in Banus early one evening, she had noticed that the window model was dressed in tights matching the sea fairy's dress!

One Monday morning Gerri, whose exquisite water coloured flowers were finely outlined with black felt tipped pen, showed Lucy and Elaine the threads she had purchased at the local Chinese store. Admiring the finished picture of hollyhocks with its thread leaves and yarn stems, Elaine gazed into the picture, "Just look at this! Aren't you clever? I could never do this. How do you know where to start?"

But her creative talents shone through her beautifully sketched Shetland ponies and love birds nestled on a dingle tree branch. Both were exquisitely and meticulously executed in soft pastels. Standing behind Lucy, Elaine delicately and very carefully turned over each page of the black photo album, studying each piece in detail. This lovely lady, with her huge almond shaped eyes and shoulder length 'Barbie' flicked hair was always beautifully dressed; her make up, a piece of art in itself. Over the weeks Gerri, Elaine and Lucy basked in the friendship each brought to the other. All three were happy in the knowledge that they could slot in and out of the friendship with their comings and goings, backwards and forwards to the UK.

Friends from home visited and went. It was great to see them and had been a huge success for all concerned. Delightful days were spent visiting local markets, local towns and the white villages and all the time Lucy's mind was like a camera, snapping away at the ideas she saw, buying the bits and pieces she needed. Laughingly, she recalled purchasing two bits of cork oak, which her school pal had amusingly carried home, wondering how on earth Lucy was going to use them. Lucy had yet to execute her ideas for weaving on cork. Having mentioned her idea to Elaine, Elaine's husband had picked up a piece of cork from the local log yard for Lucy to use. Looking at the finished piece entitled: Lichen and Moss, Elaine insisted that her husband find a bigger piece next time! After the visiting friends returned home, Lucy would resume her weekly art group and the newly found pottery group.

Father Chaos and his daughter ran the pottery school

between them. Father Chaos, appropriately named, was in his seventies and had a head full of hair which was combed back and crimped in style to shoulder length. He had a chart on the wall entitled Father's Rants! Before coffee time, he would disappear and reappear with a Simon Don's carton of vino tinto, which he would sip for medicinal reasons. Being an experienced potter, he took charge of the wheel and insisted that to succeed, one must listen carefully.

During the first morning, Father Chaos sidled alongside Lucy and asked her where she was from. Much to her surprise, he knew Stockport well, having driven the 192 bus from Manchester to Hazel Grove. Her first pottery piece was a dish made in a mould which now stood proudly on the glass shelves in their newly repainted apartment which was becoming an ever growing gallery, playing host to Lucy and Sam's increasing work.

Each evening, feeling enthused and fired up, Lucy would sit and finish art work upon art work. Her collection of threads grew and grew, as did her collection of boxes. She produced a further five pieces called: Fiery Sunset, Struggling Coral, Peeping Spring, Beach Debris and Spanish Sky.

The final five pieces were called: Late Summer, Early Autumn, Caught In The Net, Tangled Rose, Spring Carpet and Playful Mists.

Looking at the increasing collection of pictures in the photo album, she was reminded of Elaine asking her what she was planning to do with the pictures, especially as the bulk of all fifteen pictures had made the album impossible to close!

The problem had been solved when Lucy, on one of her numerous shopping jaunts, had bought a splendid piece in which to mount all fifteen pieces! The item purchased was a screen made up of three hinged panels and each panel consisted of five vertical photograph frames. Sam sawed off the legs, separated the panels and mounted each of the individual frames on the wall. In order to fit the pictures into the frames, Lucy had had to trim each one. With the bits of pictures left over, Lucy designed and made a vibrant orange collage entitled, Seasoned Bottles. Both Sam and Lucy were thrilled to bits when their friends from next door had come round and noted the terrific changes they had made and how modern the apartment looked, whilst observing the orange collage with amused interest.

Seasoned Bottles was aptly named because each week Lucy brought home from the pottery studio bags of fruit consisting of kumquats, limes and lemons, all freshly hand picked from the fruit trees in Father Chaos's orchard. Wearing the apron appropriately labelled, 'Domestic Goddess', she made: lime and lemon curd, lime cheesecake with mascarpone cheese, lime drizzled cake and a superb lime and lemon soaked fruit shortbread drizzled with tangy citrus icing. This was followed by Lucy's 'Morrocquat Marmalade' or chutney made from kumquats, sugar, orange, lemon, star of anise and orange blossom water. Bottles of all sizes were saved, washed, filled and labelled. Oranges were squeezed and used in tasty spicy tagines or pig's cheeks casseroles. As the art and pottery groups sampled all of Lucy's cookery delights, more fruit would appear for Lucy to work her magic on.

Lucy entertained her friends. She tried the golf; she walked each Tuesday along the seafront with her girlfriends; she made arrangements with her walking pal, Sue, to meet up at Jerez to watch the motor racing and invited her to her chalet in Wales. She tried crown green bowling and was instructed by Graham, who had partnered the famous bowler David Bryant. She'd found out about the local jive and shooting groups but hadn't had time to investigate! She had started the swimming but had given up because of the early start in the dark mornings. So much to do and so little time to do it all in!

And NADFAS, the local fine arts group, had as always entertained them with lectures, even though Sam's snores were heard on the back row by friends five rows in front! Through the society they had met some wonderful friends who had accompanied them one Sunday afternoon to the

Benahavis Hotel where there was a superb exhibition of over 50 local artists. Lucy had noted the artist who painted vibrant sea scenes of octopus, crab, squid and fish on glass. It was from him that she had found the inspiration for her four pottery sea tiles consisting of a crab, an octopus, a jellyfish and a seahorse. She remembered a particular day at pottery when she had struggled to transform her paper design into clay; she had become extremely frustrated and was on the point of giving up when, within the clay, a sea horse emerged. Everyone admired the beautifully sculptured and delicate creature. Remembering Father Chaos calling her an artist, her mind flooded with ideas for sea mobiles, tiled wall scenes, a plethora of pots and the sea gull which her friend had texted her. Next visit she would make that gull as well!

The acrylics Lucy would also master on her next visit, as she loved their textural feel. Remembering her last visit to the art group, she had arrived armed with jars of 'Morrocquat' which Val sold to eager buyers. She had met up with Norma, who being in remission from cancer, had discussed wigs with Lucy. Both of them came to the conclusion that even wearing a wig could be a form of art!

It was now two days short of the three months and, although ready to return home, Lucy didn't plan to take any work with her. The pieces belonged to Spain. Admitting that she hadn't, as suspected by those sceptics in the UK, just endured her sojourn, but positively immersed herself into a way of life which had rekindled her creativity. The people Lucy had met reminded her of different works of art, whether they were sketched in pencil or charcoal, painted in oils or watercolours, acrylics or pastels or decorated with threads and ribbons. Having experienced and been awakened to so many colours, tastes and flavours, Lucy wondered how long she would be able to stay in the UK without returning to Spain?

Viva Espana!

A Lesson in Life

"Just get in the car will you?"

"Don't want to."

"Please, Seb, just for once, please don't make a battle of this."

Her voice is rising, pleading, as he wonders just how far he can push her buttons today.

Seb stands defiant: fists clenched, back straight, blonde cherubic curls and bright, piercing blue eyes staring at her with a defiance which is almost incredible even in a four year old.

Samantha, his sister, older by only 18 months sits demurely in her booster seat, safety belt already done up, clutching her bright, new swimming bag, a recent birthday acquisition complete with goggles, cap and drink, all assembled by herself.

Quietly, she asserts herself in this very well rehearsed drama which takes place every Tuesday afternoon at ten minutes to five if they are lucky or five minutes to five if Seb is being particularly awkward, as he is today.

52

Very quietly, she says, "Mummy, I'm going to be late for my swimming lesson."

"Shut up you!" her brother shouts. "I don't want to go, I never want to go to your stupid swimming lesson. Why can't I just stay here?"

Carol inhales deeply, trying to meet the needs of her completely opposite children. Count to ten she thinks in her head; don't let him get to you.

"You know perfectly well why not, Seb," she says calmly, firmly, but there is a dangerous undertone to his mother's voice now which Seb recognises, indicating that he was draining her patience.

"We go through this every week. I can't leave you here on your own."

"Why not?"

"Because you are too young."

"Am not. Why can't Daddy look after me?"

"Because," she hesitates, taking another deep breath, delivering this well rehearsed line, the script known off by heart by all three players, "Daddy won't be home for at least another hour."

Finally, her patience snaps, "Get – in - the - bloody - car - NOW!"

The edge in her voice alerts him to the fact that, once again, he has somehow managed to upset her and he jumps into the car at a speed which amazes all three of them and sits with his arms tightly crossed, containing all his pent up anger, whilst his mother, recognising that she needs to make the most of this rare compliance, snaps the belt of the matching booster seat beside his sister's at an equally amazing speed.

"Thank you," Carol says.

"Thank YOU," Seb barks from the back, and gives a slight kick to the back of his mother's seat.

Carol knows to ignore this, but Samantha, quiet for so long, says, "Mummy, Seb's just kicked the seat."

"I know, darling," Carol sings out sarcastically as she puts the key into the ignition, "but we're going to ignore him aren't we or we won't get to your swimming lesson at all."

Samantha recognises that a response isn't necessary to the rhetorical question, but she turns, safely out of her mother's gaze and pulls out her tongue sharply at her brother who replies with an even deeper kick to the back of his mother's seat.

"She's just pulled her tongue out at me. What are YOU going to do about that?" he shouts from the back of the car.

"I'll tell you what I'm going to do about that. I'm going to ignore that as well."

Carol slams the car into reverse and takes off sharply backwards only to be greeted by an equally alarming thump from the back wheel as she hits a soft but sizeable, unknown object.

"What was that?" Samantha asks.

Carol unfastens her safety belt and flinging open the driver's door peers towards the back wheel, where the much loved and somewhat ancient family tabby cat lies, twitching and jerking violently on the ground underneath the back bumper of the car. Carol clutches her hand to her mouth and, for once, there is a deafening silence from the back of the car as both children instinctively recognise that something truly awful has happened. They have not previously rehearsed this part of the Tuesday night drama; there are no recognised responses, no known lines.

Carol raises her hand and points towards Seb with as much parental force as she can muster, "Stay in the car!"

54

She moves towards the writhing body of the cat whose pink tongue hangs out alarmingly, her eyes ridiculously large with pain and fear.

She kneels beside the prostrate cat. There are no visible marks. Perhaps, she thinks unreasonably, the cat can be saved if she can just get her to the vets on time. It is then that she is aware of Seb, who, as usual, had to defy his mother's clear instruction to stay in the car by getting out. He stands beside her as his voice begins to rise alarmingly, "AaaaaAAAAAAAG! You've hurt Tigsy. You've hurt Tigsy!"

"Seb, please, I didn't do it deliberately, try to be quiet, you are upsetting her and she's hurt, we need to keep calm."

"You cat murderer, you!" he screams inconsolably and with that, the cat manages to raise itself and veer off sharply to a bush at the far end of the drive, once again quite unreasonably raising everyone's hopes that perhaps it is saveable.

By now, Samantha has also joined her brother on the drive, subconsciously recognising that today's swimming lesson is doomed.

With tearful sobs, Samantha, blurts out, "Mummy, you have to help her."

"I know, I know, but now I have to find her."

Miraculously, even Seb is shocked into quiet, perhaps realising that his screams weren't actually helping the situation. The three participants creep about quietly trying to find exactly where the cat is hidden in the dense undergrowth of bushes.

"Tigsy," calls out Carol, softly.

"Chsch, chsch, chsch," calls Samantha with outstretched hands, the call used to find the cat whenever it is hidden in the house, usually trying to evade Seb's screams or temper tantrums.

55

"Tigsy, Tigsy, Tigsy," calls Seb, a little too loud to console an injured and hurt animal.

Finally, Carol manages to locate the gasping cat and reaching in, she gently extricates her from the scratching and clutching bushes. She holds her closely, carefully, but recognises from her long experience of being around animals that, although the cat is unmarked, it has finally used up all of its nine lives, despite having lasted for almost seventeen years. No vet can save Tigsy and she knows it only too well. To put her in the car and drive to the vets would be an act of cruelty in itself. Ah, Tigsy, she thinks, as she gently soothes and strokes the soft striped fur so loved for so many years, why did you have to run under that wheel at that split second today?

Holding back the tears pinching at the back of her eyes, Carol gently and quietly carries the cat towards the house where, somewhere on the way, she eventually becomes still and even softer in her arms.

The children quietly follow.

When they reach the house, Samantha and Seb watch as their mother takes up the large, faded blue comforter from the back of the chair. Tatty, but loved, it seems an appropriate resting place for the body of the cat. Placing it down on the carpet, she places the limp and lifeless body on top of it. The eyes lie still and horribly dead beneath the lids.

Samantha gently touches her mother's arm, shaking her out of her torpor,

"Can you make her better, Mummy?"

She thinks of all the baby birds found in the Spring, the lambs in the field, half eaten by foxes, the dead badger at the side of the road last year, but knows that this is the first death that will actually mean anything real to the children. Samantha will cope; she is practical, sensible, balanced with a rationality belying her just six year old self. It is Seb, this emotional and exceptionally intelligent child who Carol fears for and it is to him she turns towards, holding out her arms for him to run into.

"No, I'm sorry, darling," she says, as she pulls Samantha in as well into what has now become a communal hug.

"You didn't mean to do it, did you, Mummy?" Seb asks.

"No, darling."

"But why did she do that? Why did she run under the car?"

"I don't know, Seb, there aren't always answers for everything."

"Is she dead?" he mews quietly.

"Yes," Carol answers.

"She was very old," Samantha says, diplomatically. "Perhaps she didn't see the car."

"Perhaps not," says Carol.

All three stand around the lifeless body of the cat until Carol shakes herself into becoming the horribly responsible adult in every sense of the word. She sniffs and wipes the back of her hand across her nose.

"I'm just going to get a cardboard box from the garage to put her in."

"Why?" says Seb.

"Because she can't stay here, Seb."

"Why not? Why can't she stay here?"

"Tigsy's gone."

"Where's she gone?"

"She's gone to Heaven, hasn't she Mummy?" says Samantha.

"Yes, that's right, Samantha, she's gone to Heaven," says

Carol gratefully. "Later on when Daddy comes home we will find her a nice place in the garden to rest, where we can bury her."

"Why?" asks Seb.

"Because that's what we do when something or someone dies, Seb."

"Why? Why can't she stay here with us?"

Carol ignores this last question and goes off to the garage to find a box of suitable size in which to place the cat.

When she returns, both children are crouched somewhat tentatively but very tenderly by the cat, Seb gently strokes her back, whilst Samantha gently strokes the top of her head. Carol looks on and draws a deep breath before kneeling down, lifting the body and placing it gently in the box along with the old comforter.

"Say goodbye before I cover her up and we leave her in peace."

"We should say a prayer," Samantha says. "Isn't that what we should do?"

"Yes, of course we can," says Carol tenderly. "That's a lovely idea, Sam."

Suddenly, Seb springs to his feet.

"Please, Mummy, let me do it. I know a prayer. Please let me do it!"

"All right. You can say a prayer when I've covered her up," says Carol proudly, thinking, at last he is calm, her love for him springing up so strong, despite the horror of the last ten minutes.

All three of them gently pull the cover over the cat, tucking it in for its final sleep.

It is at this point that, Seb, ridiculously pleased with himself for having been appointed to the task of saying the prayer, leaps up and down in the air in the most enthusiastic and most inappropriately wild manner imaginable, shouting loudly like some Massai warrior with his hands bouncing up and down with each increasingly higher and bouncier movement:

"For (JUMP) what (JUMP) we are about to receive (JUMP, JUMP) may the Lord make us truly thankful (JUMP)!"

Samantha stares in horror. Carol draws herself up large and, clenching her teeth lurches for Seb across the box containing the cat, with well practised skill, "You little……!"

Seb senses, only now, that the prayer perhaps wasn't the right one to match the solemnity of the occasion and leaps neatly out of the clutches of his mother, screaming even more loudly, "It's not my fault! That's the only prayer we ever say at nursery." Bawling loudly, he makes a quick exit to his bedroom.

Later that evening, when Dad has come home and the cat has been ceremoniously buried under the old apple tree in a quiet corner of the garden, Seb lies in bed, finally forgiven, listening to his favourite bedtime story read to him by his mother who by now is exhausted. She is used to busy days with regular challenges and battles, but today's has been exceptional by even their standards.

"Mummy?" he asks, gently.

"Yes, Seb," Carol responds, peace finally restored, "just one more question, only one and then you really are going to go to sleep. Agreed?"

"Agreed," he says. Turning his face towards his mother, he places both hands on either side of her face and asks very quietly. "You know we have a nature table at nursery?"

"Yes," answers Carol.

"And you know Mrs Smith says that we can bring things in

to show that we find?"

"Ye..es," Carol was beginning to wonder where he was going with this question, which as usual was turning into a string of questions.

"And you know Daddy said that Tigsy will turn to bones?"

"Ye..e..es."

"Do you think we can dig her up and I can take her in for the nature table?"

With that, Carol gets up and turns off the light.

"Goodnight, Seb," she says firmly.

"Goodnight, Mummy," responds Seb, knowing that, once again, he just might have said the wrong thing and he had very firmly used up all his questions for that day.

"Night night, Seb."

"Night night, Mummy, and night night, Tigsy," she hears him say very softly as she pulls the bedroom door to.

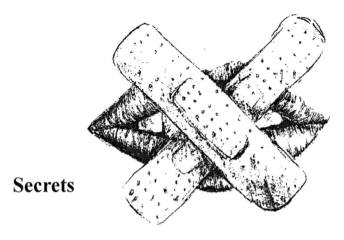

Secrets

Ruth missed both her parents.

Ruth thought of her mother as a folded blanket which she occasionally lifted, ever so carefully, from the cupboard shelf. Holding both corners she would vigorously shake the blanket loose but still the creases remained. Although Ruth tried to mentally iron them out, they were stubbornly fixed within the softness of the blanket. Instead of providing a welcoming, warm covering for Ruth's body and soul, the blanket was always carefully folded, smoothed flat and returned to its shelf.

It was one of those days for reminiscing and Ruth had spread the black and white photographs of her parents across the coffee table. She noticed that her mother's eyes never looked into the camera, always gazing elsewhere into the distance. Even then, her mother seemed to be harbouring her own secret thoughts, longings and desires.

It was a summer in the late sixties when Ruth, struggling through the usual merry go round of adolescence, had noticed a change in her mother's behaviour. In front of her friends, mum would often parade around the family home in bra and pants which Ruth didn't find embarrassing, just rather confusing. There were other incidences that also perplexed

61

her. It was only the previous day when her mother, having parked the car whilst waiting to pick up Ruth from school, had watched her approach and commented on her 'lupin' legs! Did her mother have to comment on her body when Ruth had to witness her mother's lingerie display every other day? It wasn't that Ruth found her mum unattractive, quite the opposite, but what was wrong with Ruth's legs? Couldn't her mother understand how sensitive she already was to what girls of her age supposed their required body image should be? Furthermore, Ruth recoiled, as the image of next door's lupin flowers painted an indelible picture in her mind.

"What do lupin legs mean?" asked Ruth sat next to mum in the car.

"Straight up and down," she replied.

"Oh!"

It was shortly afterwards that Ruth had noticed the strange behaviour of the next door neighbour Mr. Poole. He had always come across as a rather fresh faced, insignificant little man who was prematurely balding. Each day donning a city suit and bowler hat he hurriedly 'bobbed' along to the station; hailing each of his fellow man on route with raised umbrella or briefcase. Today was Saturday and he was furtively hiding behind the hedge, ogling Ruth's mother whilst she hung out the washing in her couture of nearly naked attire.

Michael Poole is that you behind that hedge?

Michael Poole turned bright red and flew in doors leaving mother somewhat bemused at his very obvious feelings of embarrassment. He had been spotted! But who could blame Mr Poole when Ruth remembered her mother's wonderful long model legs? Those infamous legs which were the topic of conversation one evening in the country pub! As Ruth walked into The Dog and Duck she couldn't ignore the obese and drunken local farmer loudly holding forth, divulging his lascivious memory to an enthralled audience. His huge belly shook, his eyes widened with excitement as he gesticulated wildly with his hands. Alternately mopping his brow with one hand and taking huge gulps of bitter with the other, which having missed his mouth glistened on his huge jowls and dripped onto his hairy open shirted chest, there could be no mistake about who had aroused such an ardent passion:

"And those legs they just went on and on. I tell you … (he noticed Ruth) I tell you, your mother's legs going over that stile …well I said, I tell you I said, do you need a hand there? I'd be more than obliging! Wonderful! Bloody wonderful!"

Had Ruth secretly envied her mother or was she, ever so slightly, taken aback by the fact that another man had found her mother sexually arousing? For God's sake she was her mother not a teenager! There seemed to be some kind of role reversal happening.

On another occasion she noticed her mother with her friend Chris. He arrived unannounced whilst Ruth was out. Perching himself on the kitchen bar stool drinking tea, he spent endless hours chatting to mum who sat opposite him with those long stilted legs stretched out as she leant her body against the kitchen wall and became Claire Rayner - the Agony Aunt! Or could it have been that last time, when mum had insisted that Ruth's latest boyfriend sat still for hours, either in the freezing cold or the frazzling heat of the glass logia, whilst she finished his portrait? How many hours had she sat gazing at him and him at her?

Ruth had loved her mother. In conversation with friends her mum had been described as rather eccentric, rather charming and definitely refreshing in comparison to their 'twinset and pearls' or 'meat and two veg.' mums. One friend, being rather on the large size, loved being invited to the house for tea because in her words - there was never much to eat!

Consequently, she was able to forego her mother's enormous portions and lose weight. It wasn't that Ruth's mother couldn't cook. She just wasn't interested. If only things had been boring and predictable. But far from it!

It was the summer of '71 and Ruth was seventeen. She remembered and noted every detail of where and how the thunderbolt of the 'secret' had been broken to her.

Approaching the junction after passing the park gates from Richmond Road, Ruth recalled how earlier that day she had been walking to her grandparent's house to meet her mum and had decided to cut through the park. Once inside, she had been confronted by a gang of girls who had secretly hidden themselves underneath the rhododendron bushes surrounding the bowling green. They emerged like an ugly dark huddled line of a twisted oil slick spilling out into Ruth's path. Ridiculing Ruth's convent uniform, which she also utterly detested, they commanded her to strip! Ruth remembered the angry bubble starting to swell and rise in the pit of her belly. It erupted with a few specially chosen words and after flinging her hat to the ground, she put up her fists with the very serious intention of hurting someone. The admonished girls skulked away. Driving past the park gates, Ruth wonderered whether the menacing trio were hiding in the same bushes awaiting their next   unsuspecting victim. Surely her mother would be proud of her daughter standing up to this gang? She was just about to relate the incident when her mum in a hesitant and nervous voice asked:

"Can you keep a secret, Ruth? I don't know whether I should tell you or not. I hope you will understand and still love me."

Of course Ruth had understood. Why wouldn't she? Wasn't she hopelessly in love with her boyfriend? Hadn't she spent hours writing love poems in her best ink pen, re-reading each word until she knew them off by heart? Ruth knew what it felt like to be in love! If her mother felt as she did what could she say. Asking her mother whether she was sure, her mother answered with a positive and affirmative yes!

Mum was in love with another man and not once did Ruth think of her father.

More importantly Ruth was sworn to secrecy.

Ruth had said she understood. She had never challenged her mother's feelings. Why was she unhappy? Maybe had she done so at that time, just as she had challenged the 'gang of hyenas' in the park, the outcome would have been very different? Instead, they had behaved like best friends, and one had conspiratorially divulged her darkest secret to the other.

The secret remained a secret until a few months later when her mother unexpectedly burst in on Ruth in the family bathroom. She was applying her make up. Seeing her mother's emblazoned eyes in the mirror reminded her of a feral cat as she vehemently hissed and squeezed through her clenched teeth:

"Do you know what you have done? Do you know the damage you've caused?"

"Ruth didn't give your secret away. How long has Ruth known?"

But she had kept the secret! In a split second Ruth remembered her father pulling her mother away:

Her father never involved her again.

Now she realised that 'the secret' had trapped her into feeling abandoned and alone. Why? It wasn't as though the memory of that particular day was all bad but it had always bothered her. The secret had had a way of souring Ruth's life, of colouring it in different hues. After mum departed, Ruth went to college, and because of other circumstances, never felt able to return and live in the family home. Those years at home would have given Ruth space and time to grow emotionally, to recover from the debris of a divorce, time to heal from a failed relationship but more importantly the time to reunite ties with her father. Ruth felt that her mother had not only abandoned her and the family, but eventually herself. During Ruth's last visit to her mother at the nursing home she whispered:

"I have been such a foolish woman."

Ruth thought about her own children and how proud she was of them. Motherhood to Ruth had been the fulfilment of all her dreams; it had and always would give her a lifetime of lasting love and commitment. Perhaps her mother had inadvertently sacrificed this in order to find that happiness which eventually eluded her. Perhaps her mother had felt unrecognised and not needed as Ruth ventured out on her own path in life. But nothing could have been further from the truth.

Today was Ruth's birthday, the same day as mum. Having packed the picnic basket, shut the car boot and driven to her favourite spot on the hill overlooking the sea, Ruth sat in the sunshine. Unfolding the blanket and spreading it over the grass in the sun's warmth, Ruth thought of her life today. Being happy and committed to the road ahead of her, she lay down, spread her arms out wide and reached towards the blanket corners. Holding each one tightly in her fingers, she proceeded slowly and deliberately to wrap the blanket tightly around her. She felt its warmth spread over her. She felt the protection of the blanket underneath her and smiled.

Just Another One Night Stand

I awake to find myself in strange surroundings. My eyes focus and adjust to the bedside cabinet, adorned with cigarette packets and half empty champagne glasses. My head is swimming and the memories of last night are hazy and blurry.

I turn over to find myself next to a man. He lies on his back gently snoring; his mouth slightly ajar and I stay still for some time, watching his chest moving up and down, listening to the rhythm of his breathing, the memories of the previous night slowly coming together and forming a picture. I contemplate what to do.

At least I am pleasantly surprised this time. He is not my first one night stand. He has dark, thick, wild hair and stubble that gives him a rough, bad boy look. His lips are plump and his nose prominent. His skin is tanned and his chest is also covered with thick, curly hair. He is not muscular nor scrawny, not fat nor thin. I gaze around the room and take in his bedroom which is a typical bachelor pad. The cream walls are bare and the dark, heavy furniture, minimalistic. The windows have dark brown shutters which let slats of sunlight into the room, casting lined patterns on the walls.

On the clock, I notice the time: 8:28am. I scan the cream

carpet for my clothes and I spot my bra and knickers scattered over the bottom of the bed. I decide that I need to make my escape and, gently, I lift the duvet from my naked body and slide myself from the bed, trying my hardest not to disturb the sleeping man beside me.

The cold air hits my skin. I shiver as I bend down and pick my clothes up from around the room. Although the room is carpeted, I tiptoe around as though I am wearing high heels on a marble floor.

Suddenly my one night stand turns on to his side groaning and my heart misses a beat. I stand frozen to the spot, analysing his breathing pattern until I am confident that he is still soundly asleep. I make my escape from the room cursing the creak of the door as I gently close it behind me.

I step into a long and dark corridor, quickly surveying the line of doors. One of these must be a bathroom and luckily it is the first one I try. The image of his friends coming across their mate's half naked one night stand would be the height of humiliation. I lock the door firmly behind me and suddenly feel safely alone. The bathroom is surprisingly clean for a guy's flat and I wonder whether he lives with a girl. Generally when men share an apartment the bathroom is neglected and I am used to seeing the usual yellow stained toilet seat and the patterned rim of the sink covered in circles of blue shaving gel and blobs of encrusted toothpaste.

I look at myself in the mirror and assess my dark black eyes encrusted with last night's makeup. My pale skin contrasts sharply against the black and I question who the girl has become that stares back at me. My mouth tastes like a sewer and my teeth are encrusted with thick plaque. My tongue is green and my lips dry. And I wonder why I can't find or hold down a relationship! I snap myself back to reality and turn on the tap. I scrub at my face with soap and water, working at the makeup, attempting to make myself feel more human. I brush my teeth using my finger and swallow a blob of toothpaste to mask the stale taste of alcohol and cigarettes.

Once I am confident that I look semi respectable, I leave the bathroom and find myself in the dark corridor. Now, how do I get out? Where are my shoes? Where is my purse?

I tiptoe along the corridor and I vaguely remember being in a lounge a few hours earlier. I try the first door and get lucky. The lounge is similar to the bedroom of my one night stand. The glass coffee table is covered with a pattern of red rings from the wine. I also notice specs of white powder.

I locate my shoes jammed under the edge of the sofa and I recover my handbag from underneath a cushion. Surprisingly, my bag still contains my debit card, house keys and mobile phone - many a night I haven't been so lucky. As the broken memories come together, I realise how quickly I need to make my exit. Although last night was fun, the reality in the morning of the man I have slept with is not someone who I ever wish to see again.

Quietly I leave the flat holding my shoes so as not to make a noise. The relief that hits me is as refreshing as the cool air as I step outside into a tree lined London street. My next challenge is to a) work out where I am and b) how to get home.

It is a beautiful, crisp, Sunday morning, pleasantly peaceful as most of London still sleeps, making the most of that rare lie in. I slip on my high heels and the sound of my steps on the pavement breaks the silence of the street. The long road is pretty and residential, adorned with large red brick Victorian houses. I walk for some time in the direction of a larger road ahead and, as I near it, my surroundings become more familiar. I am near Sloane Square and, thankfully, not far from home. With any luck I will be safely back in my flat before the day gets going and the glares commence from sober couples and families appalled by the sight of a young girl staggering home in her party outfit.

A sudden pang of hunger hits me and I am ravenous for breakfast: something sugary and stodgy to soak up the alcohol. I grab a pain au chocolate and a skinny latte from Nero before jumping on the number 22 bus which takes me close enough to my front door.

The humiliation will start again if my flat mate is home, which I pray he isn't. I peer through the mesh curtains of the front door searching for some sign of life and movement. I carefully put my key in the lock and open the door as slowly and quietly as is feasibly possible. I am in luck. It seems he is still asleep or, like me, didn't come home last night. However, the latter is unlikely, being that he is somewhat opposite to me.

David is a 28 year old scientist who moved in 3 months ago when my old flat mate and good friend moved out to buy her own place. The pain and hard work of searching for a new place and, subsequently moving two years' worth of crap that I have managed to accumulate, did not appeal to me and so I decided to resort to finding someone to rent the second room in the 2 bed ex council flat that had become very much home.

I remember interviewing David, if you can call it that, and he seemed fairly normal. Perhaps somewhat geeky with his thin skeletal face, square glasses and cross eyed gaze, but after my previous experiences of taking a chance and living with a stranger this gamble seemed to have better odds. Although I knew from the start that we wouldn't become great friends, I thought he would do for the time being.

The latch drops on the front door and I cringe. I'm in luck. Everything is still and only the hum of traffic can be heard through the thin single glazed windows in the living room. I slip off my high heels and quickly make for the safety and comfort of my room. The one good thing about living with a random guy found on Gumtree, is that he tends to understand the boundaries of privacy; if my door is shut I do not wish to make small talk or be disturbed in any way.

Once in my room I flop onto my bed and close my eyes. My head still swirls and I know that the alcohol from last night has yet to leave my system. I take my mobile from my bag and notice that the battery has died so I search for my charger lost down the side of my bed. I switch it on and wonder whether any of my friends will be concerned about where I ended up last night and suddenly I realise that there is a part missing in my memory of last night's events: when did I ditch my friends for the one night stand and how did I end up back at his place?

My phone beeps as it comes to life and suddenly a string of messages come through. They are from Jen. I decide to leave the voicemail until last, happier to face her text messages before hearing her voice. Her later messages are more panicked than angry. I look at the clock and it is 9.45am. A little early to call her after a night out on the ketchup so I send her an apologetic text:

Morning hun, I'm sooooo sorry about last night! My phone died and I've only just managed to charge it. Call me when you're up xx

Without removing last night's clothes, I crawl under my covers and pull my knees towards me into a ball. There was a time when I would arrive home and, ashamed of my behaviour, desperately try to erase any evidence of the dirty and slutty night, but I'm used to the feeling now and more interested in sleep.

I wake up to the sound of my mobile vibrating on my bedside cabinet. Sleepily, I answer it without checking to see who it is. Thankfully it is Jen and not my parents.

"Where the hell did you get to last night? We were worried to death about you! How are you feeling?" Jen is far too energetic.

"Sorry for ditching you hun. Feeling OK but think I'm still pissed."

Jen heartily laughs down the phone before she goes on to tell me about her far healthier morning of a run followed by breakfast with another friend of ours.

71

"Fancy going for a coffee?"

"Sounds good," I reply. "Just give me 30 minutes to make myself presentable. I'll call you when I'm on route."

We agree to head to our usual breakfast spot, which has become famous for our many weekend mornings spent reminiscing or commiserating over the night before.

I drag myself from bed and pull on a hoody and some jeans. I scrape my hair up into a pony tail and glance at myself in the mirror. I don't exactly look my best but I figure I will have to do. I don't have the energy to attempt to cover up the hang over that is written all over my face; I may as well have a sticker slapped on my forehead: "I am in recovery from an excess amount of vodka, please keep noise to a minimum!"

I figure I will have to face my flatmate at some time today, so don't bother to creep out of my room as I did going into it earlier. I can hear the low hum of music coming from his room so I know he is in. As I leave the comfort and safety of my bedroom I see that his door is shut so I fly down the stairs, grabbing my coat from the banister before hastily exiting the flat.

The large, one-legged Russian lady who lives next door sits outside on her front step chain smoking, surrounded by her usual empty beer cans and overflowing ash tray. She looks up at me and smiles. I nod and quickly decide to turn right in the opposite direction down the passage and take the escalator to the ground floor. I can usually cope with her nonsensical small talk, but today I can't face it. I zip my hoody up to my neck as the chilly air hits my chest. I take a deep breath and fill my lungs. I tell myself to count to 10, put last night's embarrassment behind me and carry on.

Jen is already at the coffee shop when I arrive and she waves at me as I walk in. I am glad to see that she is sporting her usual casual look and it relaxes me. As I glance around at the glamorous and flawless women chatting over herbal teas, I'm once again reminded how I really don't fit in here.

Even those who have clearly come straight from the gym still maintain a cool and collected air about them. I scan the women as I like to check that there's no one I could bump into, no one that I will be forced to make polite, idle chit chat with.

I sit down with Jen and straight away we launch into the drama of the previous night. I tell her all about my sordid night and the walk of shame and she softens the indignity with laughter and joking. It also helps that she too ended up in bed with a guy that she frequently tells me that she has no future with. Tod is her tall and cute Australian sex toy; well, Jen would never describe him in that way, but I choose to put their relationship in those terms, as it makes me feel somewhat better about my own dysfunctional and non existent love life.

"So will you see him again?" Jen asks the dreaded question.

"I don't think so."

I know too well after years of dating in London that those girls who jump into bed with a man following a few hours of being plied with free booze fall into the one night stand category and not the future wife slot.

After a couple of strong coffees we begin to contemplate what we should do with the rest of the afternoon. It is 2pm and I am starting to feel myself again. We decide to take a walk down the river to Hammersmith.

The walk helps to clear my head some more and the previous night is fading to the back of my mind. I realise that not only did I not swop my number with my one night stand but we don't even have any friends in common, so I can rest assured that I will never have to see him again. Of course there is the possibility that I bump into him, as London can be inconveniently small, but the chances are relatively slim.

I wasn't always cynical about love. Before moving to London, I believed in fairy tales and even thought I might meet my prince! I would watch chick flicks and dream about being swept off my feet by a wealthy, handsome and successful business man, much like Richard Gere in Pretty Woman. Unfortunately, experience has taught me otherwise and I am embarrassed by my previous naivety. How could I be so stupid! Of course there isn't such a thing as faithful, unfaltering, ever-lasting love. Now I laugh at love. I toy with it because that way I can never be made to feel stupid again.

As we walk, Jen and I talk over the events of the previous night, remembering and reliving the highs and lows. We talk about the drinks at Jen's flat before heading out, attempting to make a tally of the bottles of wine consumed. We attempt to justify the amount, convincing ourselves that we weren't "too bad". We laugh as we reminisce over the usual fight to get into the club, dropping countless names to get past the door staff at the cheapest entry price possible. Between us we piece together the rounds of drinks and the shots bought for us by strange men. We joke about the cute Italian bartender who I frequently end up in lip lock with and who always ensures a stream of free drinks. The ending of this particular night is one I would prefer to forget.

"Anyway," I say, "let's not talk about how the night ended!"

Jen laughs.

The walkway along the river is busy with families on their bikes, an occasional dog running behind them. There is a stream of runners, who always fill me with guilt, reminding me just how long ago it was since I put on my trainers. Couples walk along holding hands, some chatting away and others silent, content in the ability to walk together without the need to speak. It is one of my favourite parts of London as, for a brief moment, you could be far from the city and in the depths of the countryside.

We reach Hammersmith Bridge and decide to stop at a pub. I shouldn't have a drink as I fear that the day will turn into the proverbial "Sunday drinking session" but the temptation is strong. With only a strange flat mate to go home to, the option to spend the day drinking with my best friend wins hands down. The alcohol allows me to bury any self-doubt and loathing and make new memories to eclipse the ones I would prefer to forget. I grab a table outside and Jen heads inside to order us drinks.

"What are you drinking?"

"I think I'll start with a shandy please hun."

Jen disappears inside and I survey the tables around me. Some people are eating and I'm suddenly hit with a pang of hunger. The greasy burgers call out to me and I know that today will not be the day to worry about my diet. I always find it amazing just how much stodge, sugar and general crap the body craves after a heavy night.

Jen reads my mind and appears with two pints of shandy and a couple of menus.

The shandy is sweet and drinkable. It quickly tops up the alcohol in my blood stream and it is not long before we move on to drinking wine. By 4pm the shame and guilt of the previous night have faded and in its place I am filled with a feeling of gratitude for my carefree existence in London. I am living the life that many can only dream about – this is what I tell myself anyway.

Once again, I begin to survey the tables around me. The guys become more attractive as the evening goes on or do I simply become less choosey about with whom I will exchange numbers? It isn't long before a couple of guys join us at our table and buy us our next bottle of wine. Whatever happens, I have the verification that I am desired and, as a single girl in London, that is all I need on a Sunday evening. I have my friends and my independence and men will always come last. Men only let you down and break your heart. If I never expect anything more then I can never be disappointed or hurt again.

Just another one night stand and another typical weekend in London.

Two Weddings and a Funeral

The first wedding was a very lavish affair. Our Breton neighbours sold two cows to pay for the seven course lunch and the five course evening do, the morning "Vin d'honneur" and the afternoon tea dance.

We were part owners of a property in Brittany, up in the hills with big granite boulders in the field, a bit like Devon but with trees. We had bought a farmhouse, a barn, a cottage and two fields and, of course, a stone bread oven in the orchard that was a little building with a big wood-fired oven. Our neighbour, Roget, remembered as a boy collecting eight faggots of wood every time it was fired up to bake bread for the hamlet of three farms and the Manoir.

There was only one active farm nowadays and our charming neighbours, Roget and Emilienne, who were just about scraping a living from 30 acres and 20 cows but they had rabbits and chickens and ducks and guinea fowl for the pot. But even in their seventies and with Roget struggling with very bad hips, they still managed to grow all their own vegetables.

The grandchildren had wonderful summers there, occasional trips to the coast, just about an hour's journey away and the freedom to run around in lovely fresh air. They also had close contact with the neighbours and their animals. When J was five he was helping to bring the cows back for milking and, when asked how to do it, he said "If you want to make the cows go faster you shout, "Allez, allez and hit them with a stick!"

The eldest daughter, Regine, was married first. She took the cows with her to add to a bigger herd. We were bidden to come round at 10am for a glass of Rosé and Madeleines. Then the bride was collected by the two *Sonneurs:* a *bombarde* player and a *bigneu* player *(a mini bagpipe). They escorted her to the* car with ancient Breton music.

Regine played the bombard in the town *Bagade* and so the wedding started with a parade down the village street to the Mairie led by the town band. Bagpipes, bombardes, drums and flags, the wild skirling and medieval tunes put one in mind of the battle of Agincourt!

First to the Mairie for the formal session with the deputy Maire, resplendant in his tricolour sash, then up to the church for the religious bit, and after that into the old school playground for a mega photo, all standing up on some sort of mobile grandstand usually used at the races down the road. Next came the Vin d'honneur in the street outside the local bar, Breton circle dancing to music by the *Bagade* accompanied with glasses of fizz and nibbles.

But before long we were off in convoy, with ribbons on the car aerials and much hooting, to the next village for the lunch: seven courses, each with its carefully selected wine (*Soingneusement Sélectionée* as it says on the bottles).

By chance we were sitting next to the groom's father; I don't know how that happened, but my old man, Le Patron, mindful of drinking and driving, was advised not to drink so much water in case he went rusty inside!

After lunch we had a short pause before the tea dance. We sat outside in the cars and rested our feet. And then the evening do, only five courses this time... but silly games, circle dancing, and then young couples with candles dancing cheek to cheek... lovely!

And then "Ils sont partie!" They've gone... and so they had. The happy couple had left to go back to the farmhouse next to ours. The bride was obliged to provide onion soup for all comers, just to show that she could cook, but actually Giselle from down the road, had made a big enamel pot full!

Then they disappeared again and we played hunt the happy couple... are they in the hay loft? No. Are they in the barn? No. Are they next door *"chez les Rosbifs?"*

(You call us frogs, we call you Rosbifs!) Non?

At last they were found in bed in the spare room... PJs and nightie over their wedding clothes and are ceremoniously turned out of bed - all this being videoed by a cousin.

It was still going strong at 4am, after the onion soup, when we declared ourselves tired and in need of sleep. "But you only have to go next door," said Monsieur M.

The second daughter, Mireille's wedding, two year's later was less grand. An evening BBQ at the sports hall, but we still did circle dancing and drank fizz outside the Mairie.

Next summer was more sombre...Grandmère next door was very poorly... very, Very Poorly! Le Patron and our son were installing a staircase up to the loft, the old grain store over the farmhouse kitchen, when Regine came running round from next door. "We need two strong men now." They thought it was to move the bed. But it was Grandmère who needed moving. She was still warm!

Le Patron said, "She was like a little bird, as light as a feather."

That evening, Seraphine came over to help lay her out and then I was summoned by Regine, " You've got a really good camera, we need a photo of Grandmère."

I hurried round with my Olympus and there she was, laid out on the best bed, a rosary in her clasped hands and various family pictures tastefully displayed around the bed.

" The funeral is on Friday," said Regine.

"We can't come, we've only holiday clothes," we said.

"But you are neighbours....you MUST come... neighbours are expected."

Neighbours were needed to carry the floral tributes. So I asked what to do and what to get. A pot of begonias was expected and duly bought.

Wednesday night there was a House Mass next door, and we took round our begonias. The ancient and plump Parish Priest was sitting in the kitchen with a list of contributors for masses to be said for her soul, but we didn't need to give him any money as we'd brought a pot of begonias.

Thursday afternoon we viewed the body. The five grieving sisters, some more grieving than others, were lined up around the room, all dressed in black bombazine. It felt like a scene from a Simenon novel. A family feud was in progress, something to do with who was going to inherit Grandmère's wardrobes. There were several huge oak presses, maybe 200 years or so old that they were turning to dust as they argued about who should inherit what.

The sisters were becoming increasingly uncomfortable in their unaccustomed stiff mourning garb. I followed Seraphine around the room. We kissed the two nice sisters four times on the cheeks in the Breton fashion. To the three nasty sisters we just nodded and muttered, "Mes condoléances, mes condoléances."

Most of the participants were dipping an olive branch in the holy water and gently wafting it over the corpse.

Seraphine observed, " Elle gonfle!"

I replied, "Alors c'est chaud!" It *was* very hot and she was indeed swelling up!

But we didn't get to flirt the holy water. Why not?

Friday morning, the undertaker arrived in Fiat hatchback, with a flat pack coffin sticking out of the back. Grandmère was popped in, the cortège lined up. Le Patron was given a large granite tribute, a huge great lump of rock, decorated with a purple ribbon to carry, which said, "To Grandma From Her Grieving Grandchildren." I got the pot of begonias. The funeral cortège of a dozen or so cars set off at a cracking pace round the lanes to the big church in St Giles. Seraphine came with us.

"Where is Albert?" I asked.

"Oh, he's doing his potatoes," she replied, unperturbed.

The church was full. A local funeral is a grand day out in this rural community. A long mass ensued, and the names of all those who'd contributed for masses to be said for her soul were read out...not ours, we had given begonias. The congregation all filed past the coffin to flirt more holy water over the coffin...not us, Seraphine said it wasn't our turn yet.

Then Grandmère was popped back into the hatchback and we set off again to her home village. Another mass, shorter this time, more flirting of holy water, still not our turn. We were still carrying the begonias and the big chunk of granite.

The coffin was brought out into the graveyard and placed on a wooden bier. Prayers were said and *AT LAST* we got a go of the holy water!

And then it all degenerated into *Jeux Sans frontières*.

The family vault was opened up. Boxes containing bits of ancestors were passed out by a couple of cheerful council workmen in blue overalls. They tried to slide the coffin down into the hole... "Avancez un peux, ... non... levez un peu... arretez! Maintenant... avancez... baissez...OK !"

Enfin! Elle est chez ses ancêtre and then we got to go across the road to the bar. The family, feud or no feud, all went upstairs to *Cassez un Croûte*. We sat down with the neighbours side by side at the interface of the hommes and dames, the ten *porteurs* and ten *porteuses;* we all had to be carrying tributes and flowers.

We got bread and cheese, pâtè and wine, followed by cake and coffee (served in the same glass as the wine). I chatted with Madeleine. She had a bad neck. I had bad knees: we both visited the physiotherapist. Le Patron had a glass of Armagnac to go with his coffee... "M will have a Benedictine," he said.

"*Non, pas pour les dames*!" said les femmes emphatically.

Only the men got to drink the hard stuff!

Who Cries About Salad?

Elaine walked in sat down and cried. What started as a slow, silent sob crescendoed into great wailing, snotty, face-wetting hysteria. Her body shook and heaved as emotion from the soles of her feet washed through her. Eventually, it ceased as quickly as it had begun. She blew her nose very thoroughly, wiped her eyes and visibly re-gathered herself. She stood up, purposefully and proceeded to put away the shopping.

"Better?" her husband glanced up from behind his newspaper.

"Better," she replied and carried on putting each packet and jar away with great concentration.

"I think we'll have spaghetti for tea."

"Lovely," came the response from behind the paper.

Elaine's husband had a theory that if you paid scant attention to an unusual occurrence it probably hadn't occurred. So far the theory was working well-for him. Easing himself out of his chair and stretching his long legs he left the room.

Elaine's spontaneous outbursts of uncontrollable crying had started six months ago. Her G.P. had tentatively diagnosed depression, menopause and/or stress in some form and had offered a comprehensive array of medication to help her through this temporary phase. She has accepted the rather broad brush diagnosis and gone along with the different drug therapies. Each one had its own particular way of making her feel dreadful but the crying persisted as well as her husband's emotional absence.

Forty seven was a peculiar age, she felt neither old nor young and her looks did not belie her age. She had not succumbed to middle aged spread; she was slim and lithe. Not a grey hair needed to be camouflaged by frequent visits to the hairdresser. Her auburn hair had remained auburn, thick and eye-catching. She had always been recognised by her hair, slightly shorter now, but still lustrous. Looking in the mirror her reflection disguised the crippling sense of lethargy that lay in her bones.

Everything was hard work. Feeling tired and lack-lustre she wandered upstairs. The four bedrooms seemed excessive now there was only herself and Geoff. Admittedly, she sometimes crept into what they called the spare bedroom in the very early hours simply to enjoy the shock of cold sheets and the space allowed to one person in a king sized bed. In truth there were three spare bedrooms now.

Their bedroom, hers and Geoff's, had the luxury of an en-suite. It had been installed to alleviate the bathroom congestion and consequent rows, but now there was no congestion it was easy to get up and out without seeing anyone else. Peaceful, was Geoff's way of putting it. Elaine thought it was desolate. She had loved the hustle and bustle, especially when her children were young. It was a bit chaotic but they were all in it together. Three children squashed into the bathroom at various stages of showering, brushing teeth and plaiting hair. There was excitement, annoyance and definitely no peace.

How different now. The teenage years had necessitated the en-suite, without a doubt. She would have been late for work every day without it. The preening, hair-gelling, spot squeezing, general adjusting and that was just the boys!

Maybe Jason hadn't been quite as self-obsessed as the other two but Holly and Dan spent a huge proportion of their waking lives in front of a mirror. As they had all grown older together the house had grown bigger allowing each family member more personal space so they slowly removed themselves from each other without even noticing. Jason disappeared to practise mournful guitar in his bedroom, Holly was constantly revising and Dan - well no-one knew what Dan did but his laptop was always part of it, whatever it was, and it was never shared. Even phone calls didn't bring the family fleetingly together in a communal space it was all texting, mobile phones, e-mails, every act of communication actually an act of familial isolation.

On cue, her mobile phone buzzed announcing a text message received. What times tea? xx

I don't know she thought in response but she responded with "usual time x." Not very helpful really but why couldn't he ask her? He was somewhere around the house, why couldn't he find her, ask her and actually engage in a conversation? Who sends bloody text messages when they could so easily find the person they messaged and actually speak to them face to face?

Spaghetti Bolognese does not take very long to cook, even from scratch and without the help of ready-made sauces. Elaine loved cooking, she found the whole process rewarding. From planning what to cook, shopping or even the other way round, shopping and finding some different or particularly appealing ingredients and then creating a meal, it was an act of creation wound up together as an act of love for all the people she cared about. She chopped and grated, stirred, simmered and, most importantly, tasted her food at every stage. But mealtimes had changed too. Once her children had been hungry and ready to eat anything she put in front of them and be delighted by their mother's cooking. This became teenage boys who would eat a meal in record speed and half an hour later be back in the kitchen devouring the contents of the fridge in whatever form they could assemble quickly. The most frequent but not necessarily the most popular was the enormous cheese sandwich. The food bill had been huge. Holly, however, barely ate a thing and it was no surprise to Elaine when she announced her intention to become a vegetarian. The boys thought it highly amusing having witnessed Holly munch her way through sausage and bacon sandwiches in her formative years but she was undeterred and Elaine secretly enjoyed the new culinary challenges her daughter had brought to her feet. The vegetarianism did stick and, although she occasionally allowed herself some fish, she never let bacon pass her lips again. And then of course there was that strange bout of food poisoning that Holly had sworn was the fault of dodgy fish and from that day forward fish was off the menu too. Elaine had always thought it a bit odd that Holly was the only one who suffered but then hindsight is not always helpful.

Trying hard to focus on the present, the here and now, she turned her attention to the finer details of tonight's supper. She could hear Geoff moving around upstairs and generally moving towards the kitchen, fully expectant that food would be there for him. The door opened and his tall frame remained momentarily silhouetted in the doorway.

"What have you been up to?" she didn't even glance his way.

"How do you do that?" he moved towards her, "you're not even looking at me."

She turned her attention from the sauce she was stirring and looked at him.

" Do what?"

"Never mind," he automatically went to the cutlery draw and started to set the table, a job he did with unfailing devotion and it secretly made Elaine want to scream.

"The pasta's nearly ready, I didn't bother with salad this time."

"Oh," a slightly crestfallen Geoff put the salad servers back in the drawer.

"I could rustle up a quick one if you're really that bothered," she could feel the tears coming again, who else would cry about salad?

"No don't bother, I can live without salad."

And that was it, floods of tears, sobs, shaking shoulders.

"For God's sake, El, it's only salad, I don't care about salad." He was at a loss. "It's just bloody salad."

"I know, I know," she grabbed the nearest tea towel which made a substitute hanky. "I know!"

Calmer, she drained the pasta, drizzled it with olive oil and sprinkled black pepper through the snake like coils. Finally, she tipped it into the sauce and stirred it round.

"That smells gorgeous, I'm starving," Geoff hovered by the table.

"Let's eat."

Elaine's eyes were red rimmed from crying.

"I couldn't eat a thing." She walked out of the kitchen, leaving Geoff speechless, but still hungry.

By the time he went to look for her it had gone dark, she was sitting on the end of the bed.

"You okay?" He started to draw the curtains.

"Leave them." She didn't look at him.

She was surrounded by photos. Geoff sat down next to her and put his arm around her. She leant into him. "Do you remember this one?" She handed him a photo.

"Oh yes, now how could I forget that one."

"Look at Dan… he was, is, such a joker, little sweetie. That was the day they found that old boat, the look on his face."

"Absolutely priceless. Is this a good idea?" Geoff started to gather up the photos and place them back into the box .

Elaine held onto one in particular, a school photo with all three children grinning out at her.

"If I had known what was in store for us then..." her voice trailed off and Geoff was expecting more tears but she remained surprisingly dry-eyed.

"You can never know what is going to happen next." Geoff stood up and drew the curtains. "Come on, let's go out, you need cheering up."

"Do you know what day it is today?"

"Of course I know what day it is today," there was the hint of an edge to his voice, almost anger.

"Even more reason to get out of this house."

"I really don't agree."

"Elaine, this cannot go on."

Geoff's phone buzzed to acknowledge a message received. He read it and sent a reply. Moments later the house phone rang and, as Elaine made no attempt to answer it, Geoff did. He held out the receiver towards his immobile wife, "For you."

"I can't."

"I'm sorry, Dan, she won't speak to you, it's a bad time…" He picked up the phone and wandered about the bedroom. Unable to listen to her husband chatting away to their son, she left the room.

The conversation lasted for a good ten minutes, time enough for Elaine to have poured herself a drink and re-located to the sitting room. She still held the photo and the letter. It was a bit crumpled but she unfolded it and smoothed it out over her lap. She knew it word by word and there wasn't a day that she didn't go over it in her head.

Dear Mum,

I love you, I love Dad and I love my brothers, but life is too hard. I don't understand how people manage to get up every day and do the stuff they do. Remember I love you.

Holly xxxxxxxxxx

She had known that Holly wasn't okay. She had seen how hard she was on herself. The obsessive running, the visits to the gym, midnight raids on the fridge but never eating with the family. Why hadn't she acted sooner? It was a mother's job to protect her children and she had failed her daughter in the worst possible way. And now she was gone, an overdose of simple over the counter painkillers available everywhere. Holly had planned it, she had controlled every aspect of her life up until the last hours and her mother had been complicit purely by choosing to ignore the signs. She just hadn't known what to do. Holly had appeared so together even after the argument with Dan. He had confronted her about the midnight fridge raids; he had accused her of being a control freak, obsessed with her weight, of being scarily thin. Dan had pleaded with his Mum to do something to help Holly but she hadn't been able to see through her bravado. Geoff had known and tried to act but it was all too late and she still held him responsible for Holly's final action. But it wasn't his fault either. So whose fault was it? There had to be someone to blame, but who could she blame? Only herself.

Elaine folded the letter and placed it with the photos on the coffee table. She drained her glass. Tomorrow she would feel different. Tomorrow she would begin again, start to re-build her life. Tomorrow she would stop crying. Tomorrow was another day.

Foxes 3 .... Chickens 0

John normally sorts out the trees in my garden and supplies me with firewood for my Swedish stove. He also keeps bees, which he keeps in different locations in Cheshire and Derbyshire.

Today I phoned him, "John I've run out of honey; I gave most of mine away as Christmas presents. Can you bring me some more?"

"Do you want the firm Derbyshire or the runny honey from Cheshire, my dear?" he asked.

"Bring me some of each," I replied.

As a feminist, I do not like this "my dear" stuff, it sounds patronising, but I let him get away with it because I know he means it in a friendly way.

Two days later there was a knock at my door; John had arrived with some honey.

I invited him in. He even took his muddy boots off! Would he like a cup of coffee? Yes, he would love one. So he sat down on my sofa and started to relax as I made the drinks.

As we sipped our coffees together we talked about the beauty of being retired; less money but more time and freedom to do the things you want to do; doing jobs when you want to not when you have to; growing and eating your own fruit and vegetables, for example.

After having received extensive and detailed information about the different flavours of honey, the subject changed to our neighbours.

"You know," John started, "my neighbour, Daphne, is a funny woman. She is extremely green. She gathers up all the snails and slugs from her garden. She won't use slug pellets on them and she won't pour boiling water on them. Oh no, nothing that simple for Daphne! You won't believe me, but you know what she does? Take a guess."

I shrug my shoulders.

"She releases them on the Middlewood Way!" He continues, "You know the disused railway track that is now used by walkers."

I start to laugh out loud as I imagine the amazed faces of walkers as they watch this woman releasing slugs onto The Middlewood Way!

John continued, "She lives on her own but she keeps three chickens who she calls the girls. When she goes on holiday, she asks me to look after The Girls and, in return, I get to keep any eggs they've laid.

A couple of weeks ago, Daphne left for a week's holiday, leaving me with an extensive list of instructions on how to feed and water these bloomin' chickens and when to lock them in their shed. She even left me the phone number of her vet in case of an emergency!"

He put down his coffee cup and faced me, "Well, on this particular day I did everything as normal. I fed The Girls at 4 p.m. knowing that Ellen, the little girl from next door, would go round, about an hour later to lock The Girls up in the shed, making sure they were safely tucked away for the night!

When I got home, the wife told me I needed to go back, there'd been some sort of bother with the chickens!

As I approached Daphne's, there was little Ellen looking really grim and shocked.

'What's up, Ellen?' I asked.

'The chickens are dead, the fox got them!'

I was stunned. Just one hour ago, the world was still in order.

We picked up the sad, dead bodies of the remains of the birds and put them in a big plastic bin liner. The absent Daphne had been informed, by telephone, of the tragedy by Ellen's mum. She had given strict instructions to keep The Girls in a cool place, as she wanted to have the remains cremated on her return!

And do you know what Daphne is doing now?" John asked me.

"Well, I presume she bought three new chickens and is enjoying the new girls," I suggested.

"Oh no, my dear," John corrected me. "She is now feeding the fox!"

Fairy Friends

Our last story is written for parents to read to their children. Lila and Megan are two students at Ludworth Primary School in Stockport.

They would both like to become writers!

Once upon a holiday, there were two best fairy friends wandering through the Twinkletopeia Woods. The friends were called Molly and Jess. Molly was a crazy little fairy with a jolly personality; Jess was a bubbly, funny soul with the best laugh ever!

Molly and Jess were on holiday in the land of Twinletopeia, far away from their home town of Stockportinia. Each fairy had a special power. Jess's was the ability to disappear into thin air (she had an invisibility cloak). Molly's was that she could turn into any animal, anytime, anywhere.

As they were stumbling through the empty woods, they came across a glass bottle. Molly looked at the bottle, amused and interested by the fact that it contained a green type of powder. Jess picked it up and shook it vigorously.

"Be careful!" Molly shouted. "You don't know what is in it."

"Well let's find out then, shall we?" Jess replied.

Jess gently opened the bottle. Nothing happened. That is until Jess and Molly turned around and a giant puff of green smoke appeared! Suddenly a witch emerged from the fog and ... WHOOSH! The witch, with dark, evil eyes, spoke as if she were the Queen of the Queens. She took one step towards the shivering fairies.

"I do not like being shaken like that you know!" she bellowed.

"We're sorry, Miss, but we didn't realise that you were in there," Molly exclaimed, "we are truly sorry!"

"Well be gone then! I don't want petty, bothersome children around."

A while later, Jess and Molly were sitting in the reception area at Twinkle Hotel, thinking about what they should do about the witch they had recently encountered, when suddenly, a pretty little pixie appeared. She said, "Hello," in a sombre tone then walked passed them, leaving both Jess and Molly to wonder why she sounded so upset.

"She's the spy!" somebody whispered, pointing to the lonely girl.

"What spy?" asked Jess.

" The spy for Jazabella, the witch," exclaimed a boy, seated nearby.

Everything became very clear to Molly and Jess. As they thought this, their fairy friend power revealed itself: mind reading!

The next morning, the fairies set off on their journey to find Witch Jazabella to attempt to sort things out. They had packed everything they needed for their travels. People stared at them confused, as Molly and Jess were giggling aloud yet not speaking to one another. This was their mind reading power at its best.

As they strolled on, it became quite clear to the fairies that something (or rather someone) was following them. They heard a whiny noise. Jess made a sharp turn to see a small creature weeping helplessly behind her:

"Oh I do wish that –oh it was so-ahhh!" it cried.

"Whatever is the matter?" Jess asked.

"It's terrible! Witch Jazabella has taken everyone's powers away!" and he ran away shouting. Jess and Molly spoke to each other in their minds and discovered that their fairy friend power still worked!   So now, they were running towards Jazabella's castle.

When they reached the entrance gate, the guards were dispersed all over: here, there, everywhere! As Jess and Molly walked down the path to the huge, golden door, there was a long pause of silence and Molly got the hint that you actually had to knock on the door to be able to get in. KNOCK! KNOCK!

Suddenly, the door opened. The fairies walked forward towards the long corridor, noticing that there were spooky pictures all along the wall.

"I don't like it," whispered Jess.

They wandered down the dark corridor to a sign marked: 'Witch Jazabella' and a skull and cross bones. Jess went to open the large door but found it opened itself before she had the opportunity to push it!

"Ah hello!" Jazabella shrieked in rather an unpleasant tone. "How awfully nice of you to visit."

"Yes, well, we only came to tell you to give everyone their powers back!" Jess shouted.

The witch ignored this demand and instead took it as being a question.

"If you're asking me to give powers back, then the answer is no!" she delighted in saying sarcastically.

The girls were talking to each other (in their own little way) about what to do next. Molly walked towards Jazabella and looked into her deep eyes.

"So tell me, how old is your cauldron?" she asked.

"What?"

As Witch Jazabella was thinking about this question, Jess crept up behind her and pushed her into the cauldron! She fell and her last sound wasn't an evil cackle, but a sad cry. With sheer delight, Molly and Jess jumped up and down and gave each other a big hug.

"We did it!" they chorused.

They walked out of the castle and raced down to Twinkletopia centre. It looked very strange to Molly and Jess because some people were happy and some were sad.

"Please can I have your attention everyone?" Jess shouted.

Everyone turned to look at her.

"My friend, Jess and I, have been to Witch Jazabella's castle and asked her to give everyone their powers back. Of course, it wasn't that easy, however, we are pleased to announce that she is no longer here and therefore everyone should have their powers back!" Molly exclaimed with excitement.

Suddenly, everyone started to glow. Their powers were indeed back! Everyone jumped with joy and smiles shone all around. Molly and Jess had saved Twinkletopia! Sadly, their holiday had also finished, but what a great one they had had. They returned to Stockportinia the next day and told everyone about their adventure...

The end.